Archibald Young

Summer Sailings

By an old yachtsman, Archibald Young

Archibald Young

Summer Sailings
By an old yachtsman, Archibald Young

ISBN/EAN: 9783337410148

Printed in Europe, USA, Canada, Australia, Japan

Cover: Foto ©Andreas Hilbeck / pixelio.de

More available books at **www.hansebooks.com**

SUMMER SAILINGS

BY AN OLD YACHTSMAN

ARCHIBALD YOUNG, Advocate

LATE H.M. INSPECTOR OF SALMON FISHERIES FOR SCOTLAND
AND AUTHOR OF 'TREATISE ON SALMON' IN 'STANFORD'S HISTORY
OF BRITISH INDUSTRIES,' PRIZE ESSAY ON HARBOUR ACCOMMODATION FOR
FISHING BOATS, 'THE ANGLER AND SKETCHER'S
GUIDE TO SUTHERLAND,' ETC. ETC.

WITH NUMEROUS ILLUSTRATIONS AFTER WATER-
COLOUR DRAWINGS BY THE AUTHOR

EDINBURGH: DAVID DOUGLAS

1898

PREFACE

THE following cruises occupied several summer
seasons a good many years ago. They were made
in a cutter yacht of thirty-five tons, in which I
sailed more than 7000 miles, going twice round
Great Britain, visiting the Orkney and Shetland
Islands, the Inner and Outer Hebrides, and also
parts of Ireland, France, and Norway. An account
of one or two of the cruises appeared in well-known
magazines. But the whole of them are now published for the first time in a complete form; and
it is hoped that the numerous illustrations of
picturesque localities, all taken from water-colour
drawings made by me on the spot in the course
of these cruises, will add something to the interest
and value of the volume. The black and white
illustrations were made from my drawings by
Messrs. J. Munro Bell and Co., Edinburgh; and

for the coloured illustrations I am indebted to
Messrs. R. S. and W. Forrest, Brandon Street
Studio, Edinburgh, who first photographed the
drawings, and then coloured them by hand after
the original sketches.

                              ARCHIBALD YOUNG.

22 ROYAL CIRCUS,
EDINBURGH, *January* 1898.

CASTLE VARRICH AND BEN LAOGHAL

CONTENTS

CHAPTER I

NORTH ABOUT—CRUISE FROM FORTH TO CLYDE

CHAPTER V

A Yacht Cruise from Lerwick to Bergen

CHAPTER VI

A Yacht Cruise among the Shetland Islands

Bressay Sound—So named from the vessel belonging to Kirkaldy of Grange which was wrecked on it while pursuing the ship belonging to the profligate Earl of Bothwell—Cleikum Loch and Island Fort near Lerwick—Lochs of Tingwall—Good trout-fishing in Lochs of Tingwall—Legend regarding tall upright monumental stone near the lochs—Scalloway Castle, a noble ruin—Nearly a third of the adult male population of the Shetland Islands occupied in seafaring pursuits--Influence of masonic fraternities in Shetland—Excursion to Noss Head—Ruined Burgh of Brindister, picturesquely placed on the very verge of a precipice rising 100 feet above the sea—Visit to the interior of a Shetland cottage—Whalsey Island and Mr. Bruce of Simbister House—Fetlar Island and Burgh Hall belonging to Sir Arthur Nicholson—Harbour of Uya Sound between the Island of Unst and the little Island of Uya—Unst the most northern and one of the largest of the Shetland Islands—Walk across Unst from Uya Sound to Balta Sound—Remains of Mouness Castle—Lochs on the road across abounding in trout—Abundance of golden plover and snipe—Balta Sound, a spacious and perfectly land-locked harbour—Heilaburn, or Burn of Health, in Unst—Chromate of iron largely wrought in Unst—Buness House in Unst from which the French philosopher Biot, in 1817, carried on a series of experiments for determining the length of the seconds pendulum—Loch of Cliff in Unst, the largest sheet of fresh-water in the Shetland Islands; excellent fishing in—Burra Fiord, Saxa Fiord, and Scaw Roost—Flugga Stack and Lighthouse in Unst, the northernmost lighthouse in the British Isles   .   .   .   .   pages 174-212

LIST OF ILLUSTRATIONS

FULL PAGE

VIGNETTES

ROCK SCENERY OFF THE CAITHNESS COAST.

CHAPTER I

NORTH ABOUT—CRUISE FROM FORTH TO CLYDE

NOT a season passes by without seeing numbers of yachts leaving our shores to explore the fiords of Norway, the blue and tideless Mediterranean, or the sunny isles of the Grecian Archipelago. The flag of an English yacht has waved in the noble bay of San Francisco, in the harbours of Sydney and Hobart Town, on the waters of the Hudson, and even on the muddy Mississippi, where it sweeps past the crescent city of New Orleans. A fondness for novelty and adventure, a craving for excitement, a love of the beautiful, or all these combined, have led our yachtsmen to despise distance and danger, and to roam far and wide over the pathless ocean, in order to gratify their favourite tastes, or to vary the monotony of home life. It is, however, somewhat strange, that whilst long voyages are undertaken to distant lands, some of the most picturesque scenery on our own shores should be comparatively neglected. It is true, indeed, that the seas are stormy, the currents rapid, and the navigation intricate; that in some places supplies are difficult to be found, and that the chance of being storm-staid in a Highland loch for a week or a fortnight, surrounded by sterile mountains half veiled in gray mist, and out of sight of human habitation, affords rather a dreary prospect; but, with a stout vessel, a good sailing-master, and a provident steward, the former class of dangers may be easily avoided; and, by making the cruise during the proper season of the year (the months of June, July, and August), there is not much chance of suffering from the latter contingency. Upon the other hand, how rich are the stores of grandeur and beauty, how great the variety of pleasure which such a cruise discloses! The Orkney Islands, some barren and rocky, others

green and smiling, divided by long reaches of sea,
and full of excellent harbours, such as that of
Stromness, with its quaint old town, in full view
of the Ward Hill of Hoy, on whose summit, according to tradition, an enchanted carbuncle is sometimes seen shining at midnight—the adjacent coast
of Scotland, fissured by caves and indented by
arms of the sea, above which rise the towering
peaks of Ben Hope and Ben Laoghal—the bold
headland of Cape Wrath, with its lofty light gleaming over the wild Atlantic. Then, turning southward, the beautiful Loch Laxford, and the coast
range of mountains, unrivalled in varied and
fantastic outline, stretching for fifty miles from
Loch Laxford to Loch Ewe. Of wood there is
but little, and that almost all natural ; but then, in
autumn, how exquisite is the colouring, and how
the mountain slopes glow with the mingled hues of
the purple heather, the gray rock, and the rich
golden brown of the deer grass and the bracken !

South of Loch Ewe the scenery of the Scottish
coast and of the western islands is better known,
and more in the beaten track of tourists and
yachtsmen ; but, during a month's cruise in the
finest season of the year, we met very few yachts
between the Moray Firth and Loch Ewe.

Some years ago we set sail from Granton
Harbour in the month of June in a cutter yacht of
thirty-five tons, manned by a sailing-master and
three stout hands, having been occupied for some
hours previously in getting below and stowing
away an amount of stores which seemed, when
piled up upon the deck, as if they would have
served for a voyage to Australia. The yacht was
constructed by those well-known builders, the
Messrs. Inman, who left not a hole or corner that
was not turned to some use or other as a press
or locker. We may as well give a brief description of her accommodation : a good roomy fore-
castle, where the men had air, light, and comfort;
commodious steward's pantry ; ample stowage for
spare anchor, baskets, lanterns, etc. Good state-
room on the starboard side ; main-cabin, fit to dine
a dozen people, and more than five feet nine inches
under the beams; the companion entering side-
ways, a plan all moderate-sized yachts should adopt.
One closet behind cabin stair and another in after-
cabin. This cabin, being under a booby hatch,
is some six and a half or seven feet high, and
as airy as a drawing-room in Belgrave Square.
Some folks object to booby hatches over the
main-cabin ; I admit they are an abomination ;

but aft and of moderate size they are no de-
formity, and it has always been a question with
me whether their utility is more felt on deck or
below—they form so eligible a seat, and with a
small rail enclosing the centre such a desirable
place for charts, telescopes, pipes, etc., that I
cannot understand how they can be dispensed
with. Be sure that you have them always decked
and caulked whatever part of the ship they are in,
it is the only way to insure their being tight.

When I say that beyond the after-cabin was a
spacious sail-room with berths for two men if
required. you have the yacht's accommodation
described. She was a fairly fast vessel and an
excellent sea-boat. On one occasion we ran from
Leith to the Thames in fifty-two hours, having a
steady, strong westerly breeze the whole way. On
another occasion we were hove to for forty-eight
hours, in one of the worst gales of the autumn, in the
North Sea, half-way between Lerwick and Bergen,
and, under the trysail and storm-jib, she behaved
nobly, shipping no heavy water. She was ultimately sold to an Australian yachtsman, and made
the passage from the Clyde to Australia in 110
days. We have no intention of inflicting upon
our readers any unbroken narrative, continued from

day to day, during the six weeks that our cruise lasted; still less do we deem it necessary to garnish our story with nautical details as to what amount of sail we carried, how often we hove the lead or the log, the exact direction of the wind, or the precise number of fathoms in which we anchored. Our object is simply to give some account of the most interesting places we visited, and the most picturesque scenery we saw, especially in those unfrequented and remote localities which it was our fortune to explore.

Our northern voyage was stormy, but we passed some fine rock scenery on the sea-coast. At last we got into the boiling tide of the Pentland Firth, and afterwards into those smooth and sheltered arms of the sea that wind among the Orcadian Archipelago. Behold us at length anchored in the tranquil waters of the Bay of Stromness, guarded by the green island of Graemsay, with its white strand and twin lighthouses, beyond which towers the lofty Hill of Hoy. A few hundred yards from our anchorage lies the town of Stromness, built at the foot of a sloping hill, and presenting a confused assemblage of narrow streets and tall old houses, whose peaked gables face the bay, into which juts out a perfect medley of quays and landing-places,

affording every facility for the encouragement of
the nautical tastes of the inhabitants.

About four miles from Stromness is an extensive
sheet of water, called the Loch of Stenness, and,
close to it, separated only by a narrow neck of
land, through which flows a stream connecting
the two lakes, lies the Loch of Harray. Not far
from the high road, and at one extremity of this
tongue of land, to the northward of the Bridge of
Brogar, stands the magnificent Druidical circle of
the Stones of Stenness. Close to these stones
are several circular grass-grown tumuli, probably
the last resting-places of distinguished Orcadian
and Norwegian chiefs or princes, not likely to
be disturbed, unless curiosity shall induce some
prying antiquarian to invade even this remote
spot. The Stones of Stenness are of various sizes,
and form a circle of about 400 feet in circumference; some of them do not rise above four or
five feet from the ground, whilst the largest
standing is about ten feet in height. Their aspect,
rude, gray, time-worn, but strong and massive,
harmonises admirably with the character of the
scenery in midst of which they stand. Those
leaden lakes, their surface unbroken by islands,
their shores unfringed by trees; that wide extent

of level and dreary moor sloping up in the
distance into low, shapeless hills; and in the

THE THREE GREAT STONES OF STENNESS.

centre of all, the giant forms of the Stones of
Stenness, the presiding deities of the place,
are as impressive, perhaps, in this bleak and
barren waste, as the lofty columns whose

graceful shafts and sculptured capitals still tower over the ruins of Baalbec, in the brighter landscape of a warmer clime, and under the golden glow of a southern sky.[1]

To the south of the Bridge of Brogar stand three gigantic stones, the tallest of which is seventeen feet six inches in height, and near it lies prostrate a still more gigantic monolith of nineteen feet. These are depicted in the illustration.

Those who have a passion for climbing, or a fondness for extensive prospects of sea and island, may, in the long days of summer, take boat from Stromness, early in the morning, land on the island of Hoy, ascend the Ward Hill, the highest summit in the Orkneys, and return to Stromness the same evening. Far in the recesses of the mountain, in a gloomy and rock-strewn valley, lies the Dwarfie Stone—a huge mass of rock hollowed out into a rude dwelling, which Trolld, a dwarf celebrated in the northern sagas, is said to have formed for himself, and selected as his favourite residence.

---

[1] For a full description of the scenery and fishings of the Loch of Stenness and Harray, taken from my Blue-book of 1887 on Orkney and Shetland Islands, see Appendix A.

Kirkwall, the capital of the Orkneys, is about fourteen miles distant from Stromness. The road between the two places is excellent, but the scenery most dreary, with the exception of the pretty Bay of Firth, and a sheltered valley near it, in which are a handsome modern house and some well-cultivated fields. Between the promontories of Inganess and Quanterness, protected by the opposite island of Shapinshay, lies a deep and beautiful bay, at the bottom of which stands the town of Kirkwall. The Cathedral of St. Magnus, built in the twelfth century, and still in perfect preservation, is alone well worthy of a voyage to the Orkneys. Its tall, massive form dominates over the other buildings—fit type of the relative positions of the Church and the laity at the time when it was reared. It is built of a reddish sandstone, and in the heaviest and earliest style of Gothic architecture. The first view of the interior is very striking. All around the Cathedral there are passages in the thickness of the walls, whence the priests (themselves unseen) could look down on the worshippers below, and in one place there is a secret chamber in which a chained skeleton was discovered.

Kirkwall possesses another interesting relic of

the past, in Earl Patrick's Palace. When we saw it, it was in a filthy state, being used as a place for keeping geese and poultry of all kinds. We heard, however, that there was an intention of repairing or rebuilding it for a Town House. Sir Walter Scott observes, whilst describing the earl's and bishop's palaces at Kirkwall : — " Several of these ruinous buildings might be selected (under suitable modifications) as the model of a Gothic mansion, provided architects would be contented rather to imitate what is really beautiful in that species of building, than to make a medley of the caprices of the order, confounding the military, ecclesiastical, and domestic styles of all ages at random, with additional fantasies and combinations of their own device, all formed out of the builder's brain." [1]

A most important benefit for the Orkney Islands would be the restoration of the oyster beds which formerly yielded a regular supply of excellent oysters. There is no doubt that these beds, though now for the most part either wholly or partially dredged out, might once again be made productive if they were scientifically cultivated and properly protected. This is a matter of great

[1] See *The Pirate*.

importance to the islands, especially when we
remember that the oyster industry of Scotland is
steadily falling off, and, indeed, may be said to be
almost extinct; the total value of Scottish oysters
in 1885 being only £809, as against £2174 in
1884. In 1885, the once famous and productive
oyster beds of the Firth of Forth yielded only
£273, and in 1884 £500. In 1885 only three
of the Fishery Districts yielded oysters, namely,
Leith, Stornoway, and Ballantrae.

Yet in Orkney, more than 300 years ago,
oysters were both good and plentiful, and in
certain places formed part of the rent paid by the
tenant to the lord of the soil. Low tells us, in his
Tour, that in the inner basin of the Long Hope
there were formerly oyster scalps which produced
oysters so large that they had to be cut into four
pieces before being eaten; and in Earl Patrick's
rental of 1595, Aith *inter alia* paid " 40 oistris for
ilk 1d. terrae"; Manclett, 80; and Binns, 40.
The Bays of Firth and Deersound used to be the
principal localities for oysters in Orkney, and so
late as 1845 the former was fairly productive.
The Old Statistical Account of Scotland, published
about 100 years ago, tells us that " In this Bay
(the Bay of Firth) excellent oysters, and of a large

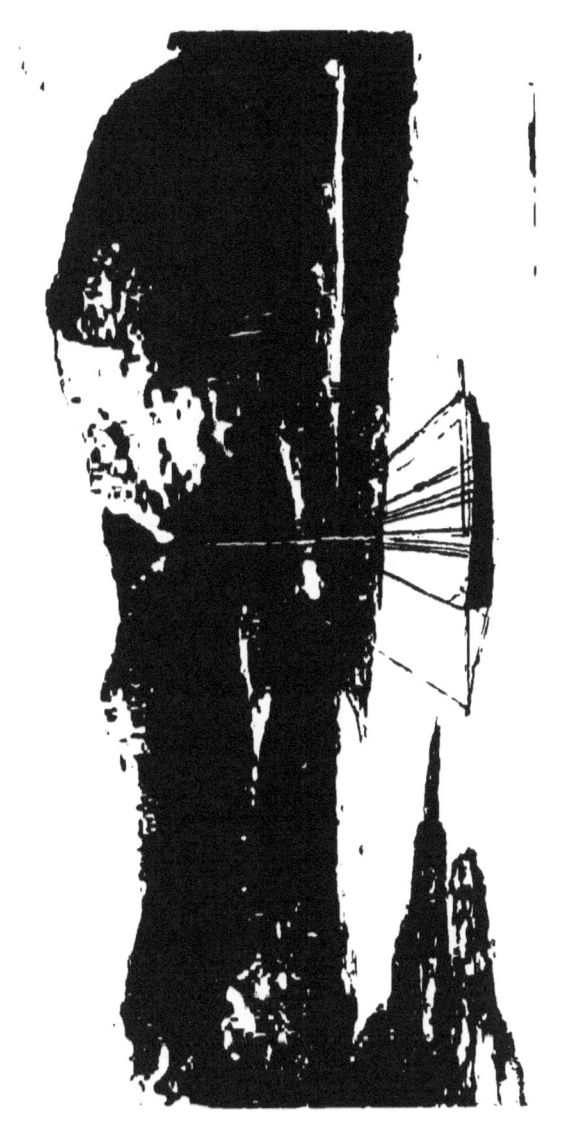

size, are found in tolerable plenty. They are sold
at a shilling the hundred." As much as £2000
worth of oysters have been sold out of the Bay of
Firth in a single season. But a fleet of boats came
and dredged them all out; since which time
the oyster scalps have remained almost entirely
unproductive. Yet in the vicinity of the islands
of Damsay and the Holm of Grimbister, and in
other parts of the Bay of Firth, and also in certain
localities in the Bay of Isbister, which is close to
the Bay of Firth, there are places admirably
suited for oyster culture, and likewise in Deersound, especially on the west side of the bay
between Lakequoy and Suckquoy, if only the
oyster culturist could be secured in the enjoyment
of the results arising from the money expended in
restoring these dredged-out bays to their former
condition of productiveness. Other countries re-
cognise the necessity of protecting the oyster
culturist, and adopt stringent means to do so. In
the United States of America, for example —
where the annual production of oysters is between
5000 and 6000 millions — they have appointed
a salaried Oyster Protector for the State of New
York, whose duty it is to supervise the oyster
beds.

Perhaps there is no place in Orkney that would be more suitable for oyster culture than the Peerie Sea, which runs into the Bay of Kirkwall under the high road to Finstown. The tide flows into and ebbs from this shallow salt-water lake, which is about a mile and a half in circumference, and which, from its position, could be easily and cheaply overlooked and protected. I noticed various parts of the Peerie Sea where the bottom is suitable for oysters. But in other parts it might require to be cultched, and star-fish, dog-whelks, and other enemies of the oyster destroyed. Of course it would be necessary to prevent the discharge into it of town sewage, gas refuse, and other deleterious matters. The Peerie Sea belongs, I understand, to the town of Kirkwall.

The lower reaches of the Loch of Stenness would probably be found excellent for the laying down and fattening of oysters, as the presence of a certain amount of fresh water and a current—such as exist for some distance above the Bridge of Waithe — are favourable for the fattening of oysters, though they would be unfavourable for breeding and spatting purposes; pure sea-water and a clean bottom being most suitable in such circumstances.

Early on a fine July morning we got under way, and left the Bay of Stromness, bound for Loch Erriboll, on the north coast of Scotland. The wind was light; but on getting into the Roost of Brackness, as the narrow channel between the Island of Hoy and the Mainland of Orkney is termed, we found ourselves all at once in the midst of a tremendous sea, pitching bowsprit under, and the spray flying over our deck. We had started with the ebb tide, and there had been a westerly breeze for some days, and it was the meeting of the westerly swell with the tide, which runs nine miles an hour in the narrow channel of the Roost, that caused the commotion which so much astonished us. However, as soon as we had rounded Hoy Head, and got fairly out into the Atlantic, the sea became much calmer. Hoy Head is a magnificent promontory, formed by a spur of the lofty Ward Hill, which here dips down into the ocean a sheer precipice, 1000 feet in height, protracted to the southward for miles, an iron wall of rock-bound coast, gradually diminishing in height. At a short distance from Hoy Head, and a little in front of the cliffs, an isolated rock, called the " Old Man of Hoy," rises abruptly from the sea, sometimes seeming to blend with the precipices behind, at other times standing out in strong relief.

During the whole day we had light and variable winds, with occasional calms, though there was a good deal of sea on, till we had quite closed in with the land; in consequence of which we did

BEN LAOGHAL FROM THE SEA.

not reach our anchorage, a sheltered bay in Loch Erriboll, about sixty miles distant from Stromness, until late in the night. The view of the mountains on the coast, and in the interior, as we approached the land, was exceedingly striking. In Caithness we saw Morven, and in Sutherland-shire Ben Griam-Mhor, Klibreck, Ben Laoghal, Ben

Hope, and many other lofty summits, whose names we did not know. The entrance to the Kyle of Tongue, to the eastward of Loch Erriboll, is very picturesque. In the opening of this arm of the sea lie numerous small islands, behind which is a safe anchorage, and beyond tower the lofty and serrated peaks of Ben Laoghal, the most conspicuous object in the landscape. We were much impressed by the grandeur of the white cliffs on our left as we entered Loch Erriboll; lofty, pointed, and precipitous, they form an admirable landmark for the storm-tossed mariner, and point out the entrance to a quiet haven.

On emerging from our berths in the morning we were delighted with the beauty of the landscape in the vicinity of our anchorage—a deep bay, at the foot of a steep range of hills, covered with the greenest pasture, broken up here and there by gray rocks. A narrow neck of land, terminating in a grassy promontory, lay between us and the sea; on this stood a solitary house, called Heilim Inn, then occupied by a canny Celt named Hector M'Lean, exercising the joint trades of ferryman and innkeeper, whose hereditary caution and shrewdness in driving a bargain had been wonderfully sharpened by many years of traffic with the crews of the numerous storm-bound vessels that find refuge in Loch Erriboll. Towards the head of the loch, an island, green as an emerald, with a narrow strip of the whitest sand marking the boundary between the verdure and the water, seemed to stretch almost across the lake; a little beyond, on the eastern shore, a bold headland, half green and half rocky, rose abruptly from the strand; behind it stretched a level tract of barren moorland, whilst the distance was closed in by a lofty chain of bleak and sterile mountains. The upper part of these mountains is literally "herbless granite," strewed with detached masses of rock, which have been torn off by the winter storms. Of vegetation there is not a trace : but

All is lonely, silent, rude ;
A stern yet glorious solitude.

About a mile distant from Loch Erriboll across the hills, or a couple of miles by the road, lies Loch Hope; between the two runs the river Hope, which has a broad, full current, but a course not much exceeding a mile in length. It is celebrated as a first-rate salmon river. On inquiring, we found that the fishings were let; however, as there was no means of procuring permission without sending a long distance for it, I determined to walk across and fish until I was stopped by the keeper, taking only a small trouting-rod and light tackle. The day was a most unfavourable one for my purpose—bright and warm, with scarcely a breath of air. I soon, however, caught, in Loch Hope, a couple of fine sea-trout, and afterwards, in the river below, a grilse, four pounds weight, when my sport was for some time interrupted by a fine salmon, which rose to a trout-fly, and succeeded, after a struggle of ten minutes, in breaking my flimsy tackle, and making off down stream. On refitting, I again set to work, and soon succeeded in getting a weighty basketful of sea-trout, with which I trudged back to the yacht. From what I saw, I have no doubt that the Hope fully deserves its reputation, and can believe that 10,000 lbs. of salmon have been taken out of it in a single season.

On reaching the yacht I found that my friend, who had parted from me on the banks of the Hope, to find his way round by the shore of Loch Erriboll, had not yet returned, nor did he make his appearance for some time. He had lost his way, got involved amongst bogs and precipices, and at length arrived thoroughly tired, and intensely disgusted with the state of the footpaths in this part of Sutherlandshire.

Next day the weather still continued bright and fair, but a perfect hurricane of wind was blowing from the south-west. I walked across the hills to Loch Hope, not without considerable difficulty from the violence of the storm. Loch Hope fills up a narrow ravine, about six miles in length, and at its southern extremity is a deep gorge hemmed in by mountains of picturesque and varied forms. Down this gorge, and along the narrow channel of the loch, the wind was rushing in heavy gusts, with a noise like thunder, raising the water in columns of spray fifteen or twenty feet high, and whirling them with immense velocity from end to end of the lake, so that when the sun occasionally shone out on them, it seemed as if fragments of a rainbow were drifting along the waters.

By far the grandest feature in the landscape is the magnificent solitary mountain of Ben Hope, which rears its lofty form, scarred and furrowed by storms and torrents, 3040 feet above the lake. Its shape and general appearance reminded me forcibly of that most beautiful of isolated mountains, Arrigal, in the north-west of Ireland. But the quiet lakes which lie sleeping at its base, and the wooded and fertile domain of Dunlui, are, perhaps, more attractive than the wild shores of Loch Hope.

Close to our anchorage, and almost on the edge of the water, stand the ruins of a small church; the gables only remain entire, and the interior is choked up with a thick growth of fern. All over Sutherlandshire the ruins of small hamlets and scattered cottages are to be found; and a melancholy sight it is, to meet in the recesses of the mountain valleys with shattered walls and green patches here and there appearing amongst the heather, showing that cultivation and life had once existed where now are only the grouse and the red-deer. The cause of all this was the introduction of the sheep-farming system into the county, to make room for which the small farmers and cotters who occupied the straths and valleys were ejected from their holdings and compelled to emigrate, so that the population is at present much smaller than formerly.

We were detained for five days in Loch Erriboll, and were twice driven back in attempting to beat round Cape Wrath. Our supplies of bread ran short, and we found, to our dismay, that the nearest baker lived thirty miles off—rather a long distance to send for hot rolls. In other respects we had nothing to complain of. We bought half a sheep from Mr. Clarke of Erriboll, who possesses an extensive sheep farm, and is deservedly famed for his hospitality to strangers—a virtue almost universal in Sutherlandshire. For eggs we paid fourpence a dozen, and for cream fourpence a pint—prices that would rather astonish a Londoner. A week might be passed here most pleasantly; devoting one day to Loch Hope and the ascent of Ben Hope, from which, in clear weather, may be seen the island of Lewis to the west, the Orkneys to the north-east, and the principal mountains of Caithness and Sutherland. Another day might be spent in a visit to the Kyle of Tongue and to Tongue House, a seat of the Duke of Sutherland's; a third in exploring the wild mountains at the head of Loch Erriboll; and a fourth in a fishing excursion to Loch Maddy, famed for the number and excellence of its trout. Whitten Head, with the fine caves close to it, would occupy a fifth; and a visit to the Smowe Cave, a short distance to the westward of Loch Erriboll, would fill up the sixth. Our last day was spent in an examination of this singular natural curiosity. The cave may be reached either by a pathway leading from the high-road or by

the sea, from which the approach is by a narrow
creek between precipitous walls of rock. The
entrance is under a lofty arch, like the portal of
some immense Gothic cathedral, and within the
cave expands to a height and breadth of nearly
one hundred feet. At some distance inwards from
the entrance, a small stream falls through a rift in
the rocky roof of the cavern, and forms a deep,
still pool in its bosom more than seventy feet below.
This basin is thirty yards across, very deep, and is
separated from a smaller and outer pool by a low,
narrow ledge of rock over which those who desire
to penetrate into the recesses of the cave must get
a boat lifted and placed in the inner pool. On
crossing this, they will find themselves at the
entrance of a low-browed narrow archway, not
above three feet in height, through which they
must pass lying flat in the boat. From this they
emerge under a lofty vault covered with stalactites,
overhanging a second dark, still pool, nearly as
extensive as that which they have just left; and,
if inclined to penetrate still farther, they may then
walk on to the termination of the cave, about a
hundred feet beyond the farther extremity of this
innermost lake. There is a spot a few yards distant
from the high-road, where you may stand upon the

roof of the cavern, a deep chasm on either side, through one of which the stream that supplies the silent, sunless pools below, leaps into the cave.

At last the weather permitted us to leave our snug anchorage in Loch Erriboll. For some time after starting the wind was favourable, but when we had rounded the noble promontory of Far-out Head, it became light and baffling, and for several hours we lay tossing on the long swell, and making little or no way. We had taken the precaution of getting a good offing, and were consequently pretty much out of the influence of the strong tides that prevail near Cape Wrath; but we saw a large brig in-shore of us swept helplessly back by the current for miles to the eastward. The coast-line of cliffs near Whitten Head, Far-out Head, and Cape Wrath is magnificent. Many of the precipices are two hundred feet perpendicular, and some of them as much as seven hundred. From the Kyle of Durness an iron face of rugged rock overhangs the sea, gradually increasing in height and grandeur until it attains its culminating point in the bold headland of Cape Wrath, whose stern aspect we had ample opportunities for admiring; as, however, we lay within sight of it for nearly a whole day, our admiration was merged in disgust, and we

heartily wished ourselves out of sight of this cape
of storms.

Early on the morning of a bright July day we
were off the Point of Stoer, some thirty miles south
of Cape Wrath, with the wind still light; but about
ten o'clock a fine breeze from the north-west sprang
up, and carried us along at a great rate, all sails
set, and everything drawing. About four o'clock,
after a fine run, we entered Loch Ewe, and came
to anchor near the beautiful village of Poolewe, at
the head of the loch.

If the reader will take the trouble to look at the
map of Scotland, he will see that an almost uninter-
rupted range of mountains extends along the coast
from Ben Dearg, south of Cape Wrath, to Loch
Ewe. That mountain chain is more varied in
outline, and more striking and picturesque in
appearance, than any other in Great Britain. The
summits vary in height from two thousand to
three thousand three hundred feet—the highest is
Ben More in Assynt; the most singular, Suilven,
or the Sugar-Loaf. Winding amongst these
mountains, and extending up to the openings of
the narrow valleys that divide them, and afford
a channel for their waters, are a multitude of
arms of the sea, many of them of great beauty,

and affording to the yachtsman a choice of safe and convenient harbours. From one of these salt-water lochs, Loch Glen Dhu, £30,000 worth of herrings were taken in a single year.

Close to the shore, and a little way south of Loch Laxford, lies the singular island of Handa, in many respects more wonderful than Staffa. On the north-west side it presents stupendous cliffs four hundred feet perpendicular, the haunts of myriads of sea-fowl. Here, as at Staffa, may be seen basaltic columns, but those of Handa are peculiar to it, being arranged in horizontal layers, and presenting an appearance as if built by the hand of man.

At Loch Ewe we were more within the beaten track of tourists than we had been since leaving the Moray Firth. Our first care was, of course, to make arrangements for a visit to the far-famed Loch Maree, by many deemed the queen of Scottish lakes. The short course of the river Ewe is too much broken by shallows and rapids to admit of boats being pulled up from the sea to Loch Maree. We were, therefore, obliged to hire a boat from a man of the name of M'Lean, and on repairing to his house on the banks of the river we found him waiting for us ; we accordingly followed his

guidance, and embarked in the craft which belonged
to him. Both man and boat were of the same
build, the former broad in the beam as a Dutchman, and the latter a heavy, clumsy affair, strong
enough to navigate the Pentland Firth instead of
the calm waters of an inland sea. We rowed up
the Ewe for some distance before entering the
lake, having on our right fine gray crags, thickly
clothed with natural wood, and on our left, a
comparatively tame shore. The entrance to Loch
Maree is very impressive : on one side is a steep
and lofty mountain, on the other, precipitous rocks
partially wooded—the lake between being narrow
and deep. Farther on it expands into a spacious
sheet of water, apparently closed in by a cluster
of wooded islands separated by a number of narrow
winding channels. The wood on one of these
islets has nearly disappeared, owing to some ex-
cisemen having set fire to it whilst engaged in
destroying an illicit still. As we advanced, a
magnificent valley, terminated by a noble range
of serrated peaks, gradually opened up on the
south-west shore of the loch, whilst, on the opposite
bank, the gigantic form of Slioch towered above
the neighbouring mountains.

We landed on the island of St. Maree, which

is thickly clothed with birch and the common and smooth-leaved holly. In the centre of a thicket are a few mossed and mouldering tombstones, bearing the symbol of the cross; under one of these slumber the ashes of a Duke of Norway.

Loch Maree is about twenty miles in length, but we did not proceed above half-way to Kinloch-ewe, where it terminates, and where its dark and narrow waters seem almost overhung by precipitous mountains. The weather was beautiful during the whole day, clear, bright, and warm, so that we saw Loch Maree to the best advantage; but we both agreed, judging from what we had seen, that, though a noble sheet of water, studded with islands and surrounded by mountains, it is inferior in grandeur to the head of Loch Awe and Loch Shiel, and in picturesque beauty to Loch Lomond and Loch Katrine.

On leaving Loch Ewe, we stood away southward for the Sound of Rona, but the weather was hazy and the wind adverse; so that it took us twenty-four hours to reach Portree, the capital of Skye. The scenery on both sides of the narrow strait that separates the islands of Rona and Raasay from Skye is wild and stern: rugged mountains and lofty cliffs, a streak of foam here and there marking where a waterfall pours into the sea, and extensive moorlands of dark brown heath sloping away into the interior. In a few spots there is an appearance of verdure, but, with the exception of some stunted and scraggy bushes, no trace of foliage.

The Bay of Portree forms a spacious land-locked harbour, on the north side of which stands the village, built along a steep slope. The entrance is narrow, between two lofty headlands, which form the commencement of a splendid range of coast scenery, extending northward to the Point of Aird. We found ourselves surrounded by a perfect fleet of fishing-boats and herring-coupers, as they are here termed. These are, for the most part, powerful sloop-rigged vessels, whose crews do not fish themselves, but buy from the fishermen. They are often very fast sailers. The scene around was busy and picturesque : the quay, where an active traffic was being carried on, piled up and cumbered with herring-boxes, nets hanging from posts on shore, or depending from the rigging of vessels in the bay ; boats constantly arriving and setting sail ; and, above all, a perfect babel of tongues, bargaining, abusing, and cajoling, in Gaelic and English.

It was Sunday morning when we arrived, and on landing we found that the service was in Gaelic ;

so, as the day was a remarkably fine one for Skye, whose weeping climate is proverbial, I left my companion to wait for the afternoon service, which was in English, and set out to walk to the Storr Hill, about seven miles to the north of Portree. The path leads at first along the bottom of a wide valley bounded by a gentle acclivity, on surmounting which two lakes are seen filling up a similar hollow beyond. Keeping these lakes on his right, the traveller proceeds until he arrives at their extremity, when he will reach the foot of the Storr, with a steep ascent of about a thousand feet before him. This surmounted, he will find himself close to a huge precipice of black rock, on the seaward side of which a number of isolated pinnacles of the most varied and fantastic forms, and of enormous size, jut out from the side of the hill at every variety of inclination, whilst between these and the precipice above alluded to is a deep narrow valley or rather chasm, strewed with fractured masses of stone. It would be difficult to imagine a more stern and dismal spot than this, especially under the aspect in which I beheld it: upon one hand that wall of black rock; on the other these rugged pinnacles, and the deep ravine between, half filled with drifting wreaths of mist, now

.

clearing off and disclosing frowning crags and yawning fissures; then, again, settling down and involving everything in gloom and obscurity. I have never seen any place which more completely fulfilled, and indeed surpassed, my expectations,

THE STORR FROM THE SEA.

than this Storr Hill. Below the pinnacles, it slopes rapidly down into the valley, which then rises gently for more than a mile, when it terminates in steep cliffs, which dip abruptly into the waters of the sound. The most conspicuous and remarkable of the crags which project from the face of the Storr is that called the Needle—an enormous

mass, nearly a hundred yards in circumference at
the base, and about as high as the Scott monument
in Edinburgh. It inclines so much that I should
think a plumb-line dropped from the summit
would fall thirty or forty feet beyond its base.
Anglers should observe the lake nearest the Storr,
where the fishing is open to all, and in which, as
Mr. Skene of Portree informed me, it is no uncommon day's fishing to kill from twenty to thirty
pounds of trout.

I got back to Portree about half-past five, but
not without experiencing the provoking variable-
ness of the weather, as the last three miles of my
journey were performed under a perfect deluge
of rain.

Next day we drove to Sligachan Inn, at the
entrance to the magnificent glen of the same name,
and near the foot of Sgurr nan Gillean, one of
the loftiest peaks of the Coolins. My companion
hired a guide and a pony to proceed up the glen,
cross the ridge, and descend upon the far-famed
Loch Coruisk. This I had formerly seen, so I
remained behind to sketch and fish. I caught
some fine sea-trout in the Sligachan river, and
afterwards tried, though not with much success,
on account of the stillness of the day, a small

moorland tarn, about a mile distant from the inn. The best fly for the Sligachan water is one dressed with a full roughish green body and brown wings.

We set sail from Portree in the forenoon of a fine day, with a steady easterly breeze, hoping easily to reach Loch Alsh by the evening; but we were again doomed to suffer from the mutability of this most variable climate. It continued bright and warm until two o'clock, when we were between the islands of Scalpa and Raasay, where we lay becalmed for some time, though at a little distance on either side there was a strong breeze. Presently it came on to blow so hard where we lay that we had to take in sail, and soon after a dense fog settled down all round us. The result was, that, instead of proceeding, we were glad to come-to for the night in Clachan Bay, close to the beautiful residence of Mr. Rainy of Raasay, whose yacht, the *Falcon*, was anchored close to us.

Next day we got sail on the cutter at six o'clock, and, with a fine leading wind from the north-west, which continued steady throughout the day, passed through the narrow channel which at Kyleakin separates Skye from the mainland. The position of this village is very

D

romantic, and every one must admire the ruins
of Castle Moyle, whose shattered and weather-
stained walls look down upon the strait. At
Balmacara, in the district of Loch Alsh, the
scenery assumes a more gentle and sylvan aspect.
Here we diverged from our course for the purpose
of visiting Loch Duich, an arm of the sea whose
beauty we had heard highly praised; nor did
we find this praise misplaced. We sailed somewhat beyond the ruins of Eilean Donan Castle,
the ancient stronghold of the Mackenzies of
Kintail, built in the thirteenth century as a
defence against the Norsemen, to whom most of
the Western Isles belonged, and who often ravaged
the coasts of Scotland. From this point we had
a good view of the head of the loch, and the
noble mountains which overshadow it.

An arm of the sea called Loch Ling joins Loch
Duich not far from the castle; a small river flows
into the head of it, and some miles up the
southern branch of this stream is the finest
waterfall in Scotland, the Glomack, nearly twice
the height of the better-known fall of Foyers in
Inverness-shire. The scenery around it is wild
and desolate; and where the stream leaps into the
deep chasm below there is no trace of foliage,

not even a blade of grass, nothing but barren rocks.

On leaving Loch Duich we entered the Sound of Sleat, which for more than twenty miles separates Skye from the mainland of Inverness-shire. Both sides of this strait are of wonderful and varied beauty. There are lofty and rugged mountains, wild tracts of heath, and sea lochs running far into the mainland; but there are also sheltered pastoral valleys and quiet bays, with undulating wood-covered hills sloping up from the waters of the sound.

One of the most beautiful scenes is Glenelg. There is a fine sweep of a bay, with several neat white houses peeping out of thick foliage, and the ruins of an extensive barrack built in the last century, to overawe the turbulent Highlanders. On the Skye side, Armadale, the residence of Lord Macdonald, with its verdant sward and well-kept policies, is a sweet spot. Nothing on the mainland more forcibly attracts and rivets the attention than the opening to Loch Hourn, guarded by the lofty Ben Screel. Its form is very noble, and from the sharp summit its outlines sweep down in grand curves to the water. We regretted much that our time did not allow

us to explore this loch, as all the adjacent
mountains are highly picturesque, and it forms
a splendid anchorage, within which the British
navy might ride in safety. Southward of Loch
Hourn is Loch Nevis, also a fine sheet of water
and a good harbour, but the scenery around it
is of a quieter and tamer character.

After passing the point of Sleat, the views of
Ben Blaven and of the Coolin range were varied
and magnificent in the extreme. Years before I
had beheld them; but then their sharp peaks
were seen peeping through wreaths of drifting
mist, or were entirely hid by heavy rain-clouds;
now the scene was quite changed; the sky was
cloudless, and the dark serrated peaks of the
Coolins and the less pointed summits of Ben
Blaven stood out sharply defined against the
clear blue. Our course brought us in full view
of the island of Rum, a mass of mountains which,
even in the neighbourhood of the Coolins, asserts
its claim to admiration. Beyond Rum, we passed
close to Eigg, distinguished by a strangely-shaped
precipitous rock, called the Scuir of Eigg. In the
distance were the islands of Canna, Coll, and
Tiree. Towards the evening we rounded the
rocky point of Ardnamurchan, which is exposed

to the full swell of the Atlantic, and where a well-appointed lighthouse has recently been erected. We then entered the Sound of Mull, passed the gray old castle of Mingarry, and concluded the most successful day's run we had had by casting anchor in the landlocked Bay of Tobermory.

The village of Tobermory is built along one side of a semicircular bay, the other side of which is covered by the woods of Aros. Near Aros House is a beautiful little lake, embosomed in trees ; and from it flows a stream which tumbles, in a pretty cascade, into the bay. Some of the houses in Tobermory are painted a bright yellow, and the natives have a strange way of constructing signboards; above the shops part of the wall is painted red, and upon this are printed the name and trade of the owner. It is merely the Mull fashion of puffing.

Early on the morning after our arrival we started to sail up Loch Sunart, a long arm of the sea, which, for twenty miles, indents the mainland opposite Mull. The entrance to Loch Sunart is beset with rocks, but, once within, the channel is clear and safe. We, however, effected the entrance in safety, although we had no pilot ; indeed during our whole cruise we never had a pilot on board.

Our sailing-master was cautious and experienced, and we had excellent charts, and these we found amply sufficient. The shores and islands of Loch Sunart present pictures of varied and romantic beauty. Undulating hills, clothed with verdure, rise gently from the water; the rocks and mountains are thickly fringed and covered with copsewood; and in many a green spot and sheltered nook along its shores are nestled little thatched hamlets, or sunny, whitewashed farmhouses. We penetrated some distance above Salen, a fishing village, beautifully situated, and almost buried amongst the woods that encircle a deep and quiet bay.

Leaving the yacht in Loch Sunart, we landed on the mainland with the intention of spending a day or two in visiting Loch Shiel, one of the most picturesque and beautiful of the inland lakes of Scotland, in which we have since, during many seasons, had several weeks' excellent yellow trout, sea-trout, and salmon fishing.

Separating Argyleshire from Inverness-shire for more than twenty miles, Loch Shiel stretches its long, narrow, deep expanse of water, overshadowed by lofty mountains and diversified by islands. Of late years it has been a good deal frequented by

anglers, who find comfortable accommodation and
boats and boatmen at Ardshellach, about two miles
from the lower end of the loch ; but it has not yet
met with the attention it deserves from artists ;
though, from Eilean Finnan at the foot of Ben
Resipol, about four miles above Ardshellach, to the
head of the loch at Glenfinnan, there is not a more
beautiful sheet of water in Scotland. For all that
distance—nearly fifteen miles—there is no road on
either shore of the loch, but lofty and steep
mountains rise abruptly from the water. Near
Polloch, on both sides, the lower slopes of the
hills are fringed with natural wood ; while on the
north side, from Glenalladale to the head, the
rocks are fractured into the most varied and
fantastic shapes, and clothed, wherever there is
soil enough, with birch trees, whose graceful forms
and fresh green foliage modify the sternness of
the scenery. At the head, where the hills of
the Deer Forest of Guisachan rise boldly above
the small river that runs into the loch, there are
some splendid specimens of old Scotch firs in
groups and single trees, most picturesquely placed
on the hill-slopes or on rocky peninsulas jutting
into the water. The loftiest mountain on Loch
Shiel is Ben Resipol, whose base occupies the

whole of the narrow neck of land that divides
Loch Shiel from Loch Sunart. From the sharp
summit of this mountain there is a fine and
extensive view of the Scuir of Eigg, the peaks
of the island of Rum, and of a long stretch of
the western sea, lochs, and islands. It is about
seven miles from Ardshellach to the top of Ben
Resipol, and the ascent is most easily made from
Resipol Farm on the side of Loch Sunart.

Loch Shiel contains salmon, grilse, sea-trout,
and yellow trout. The heaviest salmon we ever
caught in it with the rod was 16 lbs., but they
have been taken with the net 33 lbs. weight.
Our heaviest sea-trout was 7 lbs., and heaviest
yellow trout 5 lbs. The average of the yellow trout,
however, is not above half-a-pound. The phantom
and protean minnows are the most deadly trolling
baits. As to flies, we found large-sized loch flies
the most killing — red bodies with teal wings;
yellow bodies with the brown feather of the
mallard wing; and green bodies with teal wings;
in each case with a well-marked twist of gold
tinsel round the bodies, being the best patterns.

During five visits, of from ten days to a fortnight each, in different years to Loch Shiel, every
bay in it from Glenfinnan to Ardshellach was

fished. An east wind—in general a bad wind for
fishing — is particularly unfavourable on Loch
Shiel, and we were never successful on any
occasion when it was blowing. As a rule we
found the narrow river-like portion of the loch

LOCH SHIEL, ABOVE POLLOCH.

which stretches for some distance above Ardshellach, the rocky bays around Polloch, the south
side of the loch from that up to the Black
Islands, and the shores of these islands, the best
spots for salmon and sea-trout; while, for yellow
trout, the places where we were most successful
were the wide bay on the north side of the loch
where the narrows above Ardshellach expand,

some bays near Dalilee House and in the vicinity
of Eilean Finnan, the long stretch of gravelly
beach opposite Polloch, and the rocky shore on
the north side from Glenalladale to the head of
the loch.

At Polloch, on the south side of Loch Shiel,
a little river, about a mile and a half long, falls
into the head of a deep bay. Near its mouth
there is a small village or hamlet in a remote
and secluded yet beautiful valley; its only com-
munication with Ardshellach or Glenfinnan being
by water, while on the south the only road is a
steep bridle-path leading over the hills to the
village of Strontian at the head of Loch Sunart.
There are several nice pools and streams on the
small river at Polloch, though the fish seldom seem
to lie in them, but press up to Loch Doilate out
of which it flows, and in which there is good
fishing for salmon and sea-trout in autumn. This
loch is preserved, but we tried it once by permission of the proprietor, when the best fish we
got was a 4-lb. sea-trout. The hamlet of Polloch
and Loch Doilate are well worth a visit, even
though no fishing can be had. The scenery
around the head of the loch is magnificent. A
quiet, deep stream runs into it through Glen

Hurich, or the Fairies' Glen, a level, green, smiling valley with clumps of fine trees. This gradually gets steeper and wilder and narrower as it rises towards the giant sides of Scur Donald, whose lofty summit rises nearly 3000 feet above the level of the sea.

One of the most interesting spots in Loch Shiel is Eilean Finnan, or the Island of St. Finnan, which occupies the centre of a circular bay at the foot of the steepest side of Ben Resipol. It is entirely clothed with the most verdant turf; and as you look down upon it from the summit of the mountain, which rises nearly 3000 feet above it, you see a narrow fringe of gravel around the shores of the bay, and beyond a belt of water, black from its great depth, encircling the island, which looks like a gigantic emerald set in jet. St. Finnan, or Finnian, was born in Ireland about the year 575. Desirous of martyrdom, he took upon himself the leprosy of a child who came to him to be cured, and was covered with worms which he called his fellow-citizens. This saint is said to have performed many miracles. His name is preserved not only in Eilean Finnan, but also in Glenfinnan at the head of Loch Shiel. On the island are still to be seen the walls of a small

church dedicated to St. Finnan, its altar, and a
fine-toned angular hand-bell, to which great
sanctity is attached by the Roman Catholics in
the neighbourhood. There are also several flat
tombstones, some of them with interlaced ribbon
borders, and having a claymore sculptured on them.
Eilean Finnan was the burying-place of the Clan
Ranald, whose picturesque ruined stronghold of
Castle Turim—the only relic of the once great
possessions of the family—is within an hour and
a half's walk of Ardshellach. It is still a favourite
burying-place for the Roman Catholics in the
vicinity of Loch Shiel; and on the occasion of
an interment the mourners are rowed to the island,
a grave is dug on the spot, and the body buried.
We once witnessed the ceremony while fishing
on the loch. Two large boats contained the coffin
and the mourners. The men rowed to the island
and dug a grave through the green turf, into
which the dead was lowered to sleep beside priests
and chiefs under the giant shadow of Ben Resipol.

The trout-fishing—both for loch and sea trout
—has greatly fallen off since we first fished Loch
Shiel more than twenty years ago. The cause
of this is difficult to explain, for the loch is a
vast expanse of water, remote and comparatively

little fished. The herons on the heronry in the island opposite Polloch have been assigned as a cause, but we think without sufficient reason; for all the trout devoured by the herons could make but little difference in the numbers in a loch more than twenty miles long, nearly a mile wide in some places, and very deep. Neither has there been any appreciable change in the level of the loch, so that the feeding grounds of the trout remain unaltered. Indeed, although there is but little doubt of the fact of the falling off, there is great difficulty in assigning an adequate cause. We may here mention another curious circumstance connected with the fishings on Loch Shiel. The short, broad river that connects the loch with the sea issues from it at Shiel Bridge, and falls into a sea-loch called Loch Moidart. Another and smaller river—the Moidart—flowing from a little mountain lake, falls into the head of the same sea-loch. It is well known that salmon feed and grow almost entirely in the salt water, and, presumably, the salmon of these two rivers, and of the lochs from which they flow, must have much the same feeding-grounds. Yet, while the salmon of Loch Shiel and its river are among the most beautiful in

Scotland—short, thick, and deep, with small heads
—the salmon from the Moidart river and its
parent loch are comparatively lanky, large-headed,
and ugly. This difference was first pointed out
by the late Mr. Hope Scott, then proprietor of
Dorlin House and of the salmon-fishings on one
side of the river Shiel, who was quite at a loss
to account for the reason of so striking and marked
a difference in these two breeds of salmon, apparently living under such similar conditions.

Loch Shiel is a late loch, and in order to have
it at its best the angler should not go before the
beginning of June. Our first visit to it was paid
in the second week of July. In the course of
twelve days we had two days of calm, during
which fishing was hopeless, and one of east wind.
The result was, for three rods, 320 lbs. of loch-
trout and sea-trout, and sixteen salmon and grilse.
The salmon were all caught by trolling; the trout
chiefly with the fly. Our best day was 50 lbs.
of trout, two salmon, and a grilse; and the next
best, 45 lbs. of trout, a salmon, and a grilse; the
worst—the day of east wind—only eighteen trout.
The following year we paid a second visit to
Ardshellach, also in July. On this occasion we
drove from Fort-William by the side of Loch Eil

to Glenfinnan at the head of Loch Shiel, where a monument marks the spot where the royal standard was unfurled by Prince Charles previous to the last struggle of the Stuarts for the throne of Great Britain. At this point we had our boats waiting us, and trolled down the whole way to Ardshellach—a distance of nearly twenty miles. During this visit we had very rainy and stormy weather. We got no salmon, and the average for two rods was only 20 lbs. of trout per day. On our third trip to Loch Shiel, we also met our boats at the head of the loch, and trolled down to Ardshellach, and when we reached it in the evening three rods had 35 lbs. of trout and a salmon. The result of twelve days' fishing during this visit was 270 lbs. of trout and three salmon. Our fourth visit was in August, when we found the sport, as regarded salmon, much better than the previous year. The result was, for three rods in eleven days, sixteen salmon, but only 150 lbs. of sea-trout and yellow trout. The last time we fished from Ardshellach was in the end of June. On this occasion the weather was boisterous and unfavourable, and on several days we did not go out. Ten days' fishing, however, yielded—for three rods—250 lbs. of trout and fifteen salmon.

One day three loch-trout were captured, weighing 9 lbs., or an average of 3 lbs. each.

There can be little doubt that if the nets were taken off the river Shiel, which connects Loch Shiel with the sea, and the estuary of the Shiel and Moidart enlarged by drawing a line from Ru Smirsiri to Ru Driminish, instead of the present more restricted estuary line, Loch Shiel, as an angling loch, might become a rival to Loch Tay in the number, if not in the weight, of its salmon. Besides, being a late loch, the salmon-fishing on it would not commence until that on Loch Tay had ended.

Our homeward course lay by the west side of the island of Mull, passing the singular group known as the Treshnish Islands, one of which is called the Dutchman's Cap, and resembles a wide-awake with a particularly broad brim. Afterwards, favoured by the weather, we visited the caves of Staffa and the ruins at Iona ; but these are so well known, and have been so often and eloquently described, that any notice from me would be equally presumptuous and unnecessary. We then steered for the Sound of Isla, passing Colonsay, and made a fine passage through the sound, meeting, amongst other vessels, a handsome small cutter yacht, belonging to the

St. George's Club of Ireland. On clearing the
sound, we stood across for the Mull of Cantire, a
promontory which bears an evil reputation for
storms, and around which the tide runs very
rapidly. We were, however, destined to experience
none of the stormy influences of the Mull; the
wind was favourable, the sea smooth, and we
entered the noble estuary of the Clyde just a
month after we had left the Firth of Forth.

ROCKS AND CAVES ON THE COAST NEAR ELIE.

SPYNIE CASTLE.

CHAPTER II

A YACHT CRUISE THROUGH THE CALEDONIAN CANAL

FEW things are more delightful than a yacht
cruise during the long bright days of our short
northern summer, but there are many qualifica-
tions indispensable on the part of the yachtsmen
to enable them fully to enjoy the pleasures of
such a cruise. Among the most important of
these are freedom from sea-sickness, fondness for
beautiful scenery, and, above all, a fund of good
humour. No sea stock is so valuable as this last
gift. On board a yacht there are no conveniences

for being separate and sulky in the event of a
quarrel, and gloomy faces and sour looks are
intolerable, where all must constantly meet on
the same deck and at the same table. But when
the above requisites exist, such a cruise is a source
of the greatest pleasure. If the members of the
party have different tastes, all may be gratified
during a voyage through the Caledonian Canal,
or amongst the western islands and lochs of
Scotland. The lover of sport will find wild-fowl
shooting and a great variety of sea and fresh-
water fishing; the admirer of grand and beautiful
scenery will find the widest scope for his admiration; whilst the sketcher will revel amidst an
endless choice of subjects. And then, too, how
free and independent is such a life—how different
from that of the traveller by steamboat, coach,
or rail, constantly liable to be hurried away from
the loveliest scene just as he is beginning to
appreciate and enjoy it, and dependent upon the
pleasure of innkeepers, drivers, and stokers! That
single gentleman, with the carpet-bag and sketch-
book, seems, certainly, in an enviable position,
free and unencumbered, but then he must abandon
his unfinished sketch, or hurry over his dinner,
at the sound of the steamboat bell, the railway-

whistle, or the horn of the coach-guard. And
what shall we say of that unfortunate, with
a couple of ladies and a dozen packages, his
temper constantly fretted and worried by the
extent of his responsibility, and his feeling for
the beautiful merged in his anxiety for the fate
of a bandbox? From these vexations and dis-
appointments the yachtsman is exempt; his time
is regulated by his taste; he stays where he will,
and as long as he will; if becalmed, there are
sketches to finish and journals to bring up; and
if assailed by a storm on any part of the west
coast of Scotland, there is always a good harbour
at hand. Much of the finest scenery, too, in
that part of our island is accessible only in this
way, for there are no steamboats to some of
the finest of our Scottish sea lochs. Lochs Swin,
Sunart, Hourn, Nevis, Laxford, Erriboll, and many
others whose shores and mountains are inferior
in picturesque beauty and wild grandeur to no
scenery in Great Britain, can thus only be visited
and explored.

In the month of June we set sail from Leith,
bound on a cruise to the West Coast through the
Caledonian Canal. Our northward voyage was
devoid of interest, as the weather was misty,

and concealed the coast from our view until we had fairly entered the Moray Firth. What wind there was came from the north-east, producing a swell which very much discomposed one of our party, who, however, bore the miseries of sea-sickness with most Christian patience, but did not entirely recover himself until we had reached the smooth waters of the Caledonian Canal.

Our first anchorage was off Lossiemouth, a thriving seaport, situated upon the shores of the Moray Firth, about five miles distant from the town of Elgin, with which it is connected by a railway. Upon landing we lost no time in starting for Elgin, which was formerly the seat of a bishopric, possessing great wealth and most extensive jurisdiction, one relic of which we soon beheld about a couple of miles beyond Lossiemouth, in the magnificent remains of the episcopal palace and castle, rising above the reedy waters of the Loch of Spynie. These consist of a massive square keep, at least seventy feet in height, surrounded by strong outer walls strengthened by towers at the angles. Not far from Lossiemouth is also to be seen the gloomy old mansion of Gordonstown, buried among ancient trees, and once the residence of Sir Robert Gordon, who

was generally believed to be on the most intimate
terms with the Prince of Darkness, and whose
wizard fame in Scotland is second only to that
of Michael Scot and True Thomas the Rhymer.
His deeds have been thus commemorated by
Willie Hay, a Morayshire poet :

> Oh, wha hasna heard o' that man of renown,
> The wizard, Sir Robert o' Gordonstown ?
> The wisest of warlocks, the Morayshire chiel,
> The despot o' Duffus, an' frien' o' the deil ;
> The man whom the folks of a' Morayshire feared,
> The man whom the friends o' auld Satan revered ;
> Oh, never to mortal was evil renown
> Like that of Sir Robert of Gordonstown.

The town of Elgin is beautifully situated in a
fertile hollow, sheltered by gentle wooded undulations. and watered by the Lossie. Its climate is
so mild and equable that it has been called the
Montpellier of Scotland. Living is cheap, and
its schools are numerous and excellent. These
inducements have attracted many residents of
wealth and respectability, and the town is surrounded by handsome villas, with trim gardens
and neatly-dressed grounds.

Elgin Cathedral, of which but the ruins now
remain, was, perhaps, the finest specimen of florid
Gothic ever erected in Scotland. It was founded

by Bishop Murray in 1224, burnt by the Wolf of Badenoch in 1390, and soon after rebuilt with great splendour. It then remained entire for nearly two hundred years, when an Act of Council was passed, under the Regent Morton, for stripping the lead from its roof in order to pay the wages due to the troops. This barbarous order was too faithfully executed, but the ship freighted with the lead sank in St. Andrews Bay. From this time, however, the noble structure, exposed to the weather, and utterly neglected, hastened rapidly to decay, and in 1711 the great tower (190 feet in height) fell. The only part at present in good preservation is the beautiful octagonal chapter-house, whose lofty vaulted roof is supported by a single central pillar.

Spynie Castle, about four miles distant from Elgin, was for centuries the residence of the Bishops of Moray, and is still, though much dilapidated, one of the grandest buildings in the north of Scotland. The great walled enclosure forms nearly a square fifty yards in length by forty-four in breadth, with towers at the angles. But the most prominent and striking feature of the castle is the great tower at the south-west corner, built by Bishop David Stewart between

1461 and 1475. It measures fifty feet from north to south, and forty feet from east to west, and is seventy feet in height to the corbels which carried the battlements. The north, west, and south walls are ten feet thick, but the wall looking to the inner court, where defence was less required, is only four feet. In the lower part of the tower were the vaults and dungeons. A grand hall, forty-two feet by twenty-two, occupied the first story. At the time this tower was built the Bishops of Moray were not only powerful spiritual potentates, but likewise great temporal lords, and so Spynie came to be both a palace and a castle, and in the days of its glory it must have been the most magnificent episcopal residence in Scotland.

The great tower is said to have owed its origin to a feud between the Earl of Huntly and the Bishop. The Earl, according to the story, is said to have threatened to pull the proud prelate out of his pigeon-hole, to which the Bishop retorted that he would build him a house out of which the Earl and his whole clan should not be able to drag him. The last Roman Catholic Bishop who inhabited the castle was Bishop Patrick Hepburn, who died in 1573.

That the Loch of Spynie, on the south-eastern margin of which the castle is built, was an arm

of the sea down to the time of Bishop Alexander
Bar, who died in 1397, is proved by the Char-
tulary of Moray, wherein it is stated that Spynie
was a town and harbour inhabited by fishermen,
and that boats and nets were kept by the Bishop
for catching salmon and grilse and other fishes,
and that he and his predecessors had exercised
all rights of navigation. The Loch of Spynie was
then five miles long, and in some places a mile
wide, covering not less than 2500 acres. Now,
since drainage operations on a great scale have
been carried out, it barely covers 120 acres.

After a couple of days most pleasantly spent
in Elgin we returned to our yacht, and set sail
for the Cromarty Firth, the " Portus Salutis " of
the Romans, and the finest harbour on the east
coast of Great Britain. The entrance is narrow,
and guarded by two huge rocky portals called the
" Soutars of Cromarty," beyond which a spacious
landlocked basin extends for nearly fifteen miles.
We landed and followed the path which winds
round the summit of the southern Soutar; and
a more delightful walk, or one commanding a
greater variety of beautiful prospects over wood,
water, and mountain, it would be impossible to
find. From various points our view extended

over the Moray, Cromarty, and Beauly Firths,
the rich peninsula of Easter Ross, the massive
form of the lofty Ben Wyvis, and the mountains
around Strathpeffer and Inverness. The southern
Soutar is well wooded, and in one place the road
passes for some distance between an avenue of
very fine Spanish chestnuts. Its opposite neighbour
was once also thickly clothed with trees, but these
have now entirely disappeared, having been cut
down to clear off debt. The village of Cromarty
stands on a peninsula a little to the westward of
the lofty Soutars. At a distance its appearance
is pleasing; but "distance lends enchantment to
the view," for close at hand it shows poor and
dirty. House-rent is miraculously cheap; we
heard of a house with ten rooms and a good
garden, which was to be let for £9 a year.

Early on a beautiful July morning we left
Cromarty, and, favoured by a fine breeze, stood
over for Nairn. The roadstead where we anchored
is very much exposed to the north-east, and is
so shallow that a vessel drawing ten feet must
anchor nearly a mile from the shore, unless she
is willing to run the risk of taking the ground
at ebb-tide. When we landed there was a heavy
swell at the mouth of the harbour, and we shipped

a good deal of water in pulling through it. On
reaching the inn we hired a dog-cart, and started
for Cawdor Castle, one of the most perfect existing specimens of an ancient Scottish baronial
residence. It stands in a finely-wooded district,
diversified near the castle by gentle wooded
undulations, and rising in the distance into bare
and lofty summits. The entrance to the castle
is most impressive. Two magnificent elms tower
upwards from the dry moat, and overshadow
with their boughs the ancient walls and drawbridge. Beyond this is a square, paved courtyard, on one side of which rises a lofty tower
with walls of immense thickness, crowned by a
sloping roof, with crows'-feet gables and projecting
turrets at the angles. Besides this tower, the
oldest and most central part of the structure,
there are extensive additions in a suitable style
of architecture. These were erected during the
sixteenth century, and in one of the apartments
is a fine stone chimney-piece richly carved and
adorned with armorial bearings and grotesque
devices. Amongst these are a mermaid performing on the harp, a monkey blowing a horn, a cat
playing a fiddle, and a fox smoking a tobacco-pipe.
The long vaulted kitchen, the old tapestry, with

its grim, quaint figures, and the castle dungeon,
are also well worthy of notice. The dungeon is
below the foundations of the great central tower.
The trunk of an old thorn-tree stands upright in
the middle of the floor, reaching to the roof of
the vault, and close to it lies an antique iron coffer
almost falling to pieces. According to tradition,
the builder of Cawdor Castle was ordered, in a
dream, to go to a certain place and dig until he
should find an iron chest full of gold; this he
was to place on the back of an ass, and on the
spot where the ass should stop of its own accord
there he was to build a castle. The thorn-tree
in the dungeon is *said* to be the very tree to
which the founder tied his ass, and the coffer
beside it is that which contained the gold which
made the fortune of the family. Below the castle
flows the burn of Cawdor, celebrated for the
beautiful and romantic scenery of its banks. The
license to build the castle bears the date of 1393,
but the structure was not completed until half a
century afterwards. In spite of this, however, an
apartment in the tower is shown to all visitors
as the room in which King Duncan was murdered
by Macbeth, and the very bed on which he slept
is also shown, although that respectable monarch

was killed about four hundred years before the
foundations of the castle were laid. A better-
authenticated tradition is that which points out
a remote and secret chamber as Lord Lovat's
place of refuge for some time after the suppression
of the rebellion in the Highlands.

In the afternoon we returned to Nairn, re-
embarked, and set sail for Inverness. The scenery
between Fort George and the entrance to the
Caledonian Canal is very beautiful. There are the
fatal moor of Culloden, now in part concealed by
thriving plantations; the burgh of Fortrose, with
the remains of its ancient cathedral; gentle slopes
covered with verdure, and dotted over with
cottages and farmhouses, and handsome country
seats embosomed in thick woods. Farther off lies
the town of Inverness, its gaol and court-house
and the spires of its churches standing out in bold
relief, backed by a range of richly-wooded hills;
while the gray forms of loftier mountains fill up
the extreme distance. We spent a forenoon at
Inverness, where recruiting parties, flaunting in
ribbons, and accompanied by bands of music, were
actively endeavouring to procure men for the
militia, now a difficult task in the Highlands, no
longer the nursery of soldiers which they once were.

It took us some time to achieve the tedious passage through the locks, but, once beyond them, we got sail on the cutter, and swept merrily along before a gentle easterly breeze. At the point where the canal and the river Ness flow out of Loch Dochfour the landscape assumes a charming sylvan aspect. Dochfour House is a spacious and elegant modern building in the Italian style, surrounded by woods, but commanding a fine prospect over Loch Ness, from which it is only about a mile distant. On emerging from the narrow waters of the canal into Loch Ness we hoisted more sail, and about eight in the evening cast anchor a cable's length from the shore, close to a wooden jetty at the entrance of the beautiful Glen Urquhart. The shores of the loch shelve downwards very suddenly.[1] Where we lay we had five fathoms of water on the side next the shore;

---

[1] The greatest depth of Loch Ness has been ascertained to be 129 fathoms or 774 feet, and it was generally believed that this was the deepest inland loch in the British Islands. Since then, however, Dr. John Murray of the *Challenger* Expedition has sounded Loch Morar in Inverness-shire, and has found it to be 1009 feet, or 235 feet deeper than Loch Ness. Quite recently Dr. Murray has carefully sounded Loch Katrine, having taken 548 soundings in different parts of the loch. The average depth of these is 236 feet, and the greatest depth is 751 feet or 125 fathoms. Loch Katrine is thus one of the deepest Scotch lochs, being 138 feet deeper than Loch Lomond and only 5 fathoms less than Loch Ness.

while on the other side, but a few yards distant,
there were seventeen fathoms.

On landing next morning we walked to the
pretty inn of Drumnadrochit, a favourite summer
resort of the inhabitants of Inverness, and there
procured a conveyance to take us on to Corrymony, nine miles up the glen. Glen Urquhart is
a wide, wooded valley, with gently-sloping hills
rising on either side, thickly covered with natural
wood ; a brawling stream, almost concealed by its
dense fringe of foliage, winds through it, and the
whole vale has an aspect of quiet and tranquil
beauty — very different from the wildness and
grandeur which characterise the majority of our
Highland glens. Corrymony is surrounded by
low swelling hills, thickly timbered ; but beyond,
the scenery changes, and the woodlands are succeeded by the brown heath and rugged mountains
near Strathglass. The house has been recently
built in the severe style of Scottish architecture. It is well suited to the scenery in the
midst of which it stands, and does great credit to
the taste and talents of the owner, who was his
own architect. Within the grounds, a mile distant
from the house, is one of the most beautiful
cascades in the Highlands, where the fall of the

water and the grouping of the rocks and foliage
form a picture by the hand of Nature upon which
no artist could improve. On our way back we
passed a pretty place called Lakefield, on the
borders of a small loch, on whose bosom were
floating islands of the beautiful water-lily in full
flower.

In the evening, before the moon rose over the
mountains on the southern shore of Loch Ness,
we pulled across the bay to Castle Urquhart, one
of the most extensive and picturesque ruins in
Scotland. It is said to have been once a stronghold of the Knights-Templars, and also played a
part in the wars with England. The ruins encircle
a rocky peninsula which projects boldly into the
deep waters of Loch Ness, and on a crag almost
overhanging the lake still stands the donjon keep.
A wide, deep moat has been dug across the narrow
neck of land which connects this peninsula with
the mainland, and a drawbridge, whose piers are
still standing, was formerly the only entrance to
the castle. We were much struck with the extent
of these ruins, as well as with the massive character of the architecture. The archway over the
entrance, and the vaulted guard-rooms on each
side of it, are still entire. Within are green

mounds, strewn with fragments of stone, and still encircled by the shattered remains of the ancient walls. One side of the keep has fallen, but the donjon vault, in its foundation, is still entire, and accessible by a narrow winding stair. Wild rose bushes are growing in the castle court, and some young ash trees bend their green branches over the time-worn walls. As we pulled away from the ruins the moon had begun to appear above the hills, and was shedding down a long pencil of silver light across the calm waters of the lake. The donjon tower soon intercepted our view, but we still saw her beams streaming through its shattered windows —as if a bright lamp had been suddenly kindled from within by an unseen hand—when all at once the light vanished, as a cloud crossed the disc of the moon. The effect was startling; and a superstitious Celt might have fancied some old warrior tenant of the castle revisiting the earth by the pale glimpses of the moon.

One of our party had the misfortune to fall into Loch Ness in stepping from the rocks near the castle into the punt. He, however, sustained no damage beyond a thorough wetting, and the circumstance was celebrated in the following serio-comic poem written on our return to the yacht :—

F

CASTLE URQUHART VISITED

A SERIO-COMIC POEM

'Twas evening, and within a bay
Of deep Loch Ness our cutter lay;
Bill, Tom and Alick were the crew,
And sailing-master Dawson too
(A steady cautious old sea dog
As ever handled lead or log)
Steered her course with skilful art,
By aid of compass and of chart.
Darkly the mountain shadows lay
Athwart the waters of the bay,
And the clear and deep blue sky
In the lake did mirrored lie;
And within the thicket's shade
Not a leaf light murmur made,
And not a sound the silence broke
'Till our brave Commodore thus spoke:
" Fairer night was never seen
Smiling o'er Loch Ness I ween,
And yonder Castle Urquhart old
Ere I sleep I would behold,
Where around the ruined keep
The circling waters ceaseless sweep.
The moon is nearly at the full,
So we shall have a jolly pull;
You Abbot as bow, and Scott as stroke,
While in my hands I take the yoke
Lines, and steer for the ruins hoary
Of which I wish I knew the story.
Gently in landing over the stones
If any regard you have for your bones,
Or, if you wish a ducking to shun
Ere our adventure's well begun;

And, as the castle wants a roof
You'd better take a waterproof,
For Highland skies, like woman's mind,
You often will uncertain find."
Thus cautioned them the Commodore,
From out his wisdom's copious store ;
Then stepping from the yacht, in front
He lightly dropped into the punt,
Or dinghy (a bad term for rhyme,
No other word to it will chime).
Him followed fast his trusty friends,
And sat them down on their beam ends ;
Each grasping in his hands an oar,
They swiftly through the waters bore
The gallant owner of the *Spray*
Across Glen Urquhart's lovely bay.
They reached the castle, their own steps were all
That echoed within the deserted hall.
The night was silent and still as death,
There stirred not even the breeze's breath ;
Sombre and stern the ruins frowned,
And shattered wall and grass-grown mound
Dark in evening's shadows lay,
The donjon-keep showed grim and gray,
Towering o'er the lake profound
That swept its rocky base around.
The wild brier rose grew fresh and green
In the castle court the stones between,
And close behind the old wall springing
Graceful boughs the ash was flinging,
As if pitying Nature would fain efface
Of storm and time the deep-worn trace.
The moon by this had clomb the height
And o'er the waters threw her light,
A silver column shimmering

Across the dark lake glimmering ;
It shone upon the Templars' hold
And gleamed upon the ruins old ;
It bathed in light each grassy mound,
It edged with silver the walls around ;
Each shattered fragment gained a grace,
A holy calm beamed o'er the place ;
The wrecks of time were half forgot
In the heavenly light that bathed the spot.
The pale moonbeams their soft spell threw,
And silent stood the *Spray's* bold crew,
'Till broken was that gentle spell,
By words that from their leader fell :—
" Romantic, very, these ruins old ;
I feel delighted but rather cold,
So let's be off now to the boat
Where I have left my pilot coat.
Pull away through the light ripple,
On board the yacht and have some tipple,
Water and moonlight are well enough,
But whisky and water is better stuff."
    So said, so done ; away they go
Where by the rocks the waters flow ;
But alas for his garments ! alas for his bones !
The Abbot trips on the slippery stones ;
Down he falls in the water splash,
Over him the light sprays dash,
But shallow here is deep Loch Ness,
He's safe, though in a pretty mess ;
And gaily he laughs as he scrambles out,
For his temper is good and his heart is stout.
Swiftly away from the rocks they pull,
The Abbot is wet and the night is cool ;
In vain he dreams of " warm within,"
With garments clinging to his skin,

And looking like a half-drowned rat
From shoe to smart tarpaulin hat,
He longs for a pull at something hot,
But a pull at the oar falls to his lot.
The Templars have served him a slippery trick,
But he grins and bears it like a brick.
Over the waters fast they row,
The wavelets sparkle round the prow.
And now between them and the moon
The ruins of the tall keep loom ;
Time and storm have marred its pride,
But many a year away shall glide,
And still that massive tower withstand
The wasting power of time's strong hand ;
And many a mansion reared to-day
Shall fall in premature decay,
While it shall o'er the waters keep
Its silent watch from yonder steep.
Brightly through rents in the time-worn wall
Glancing gaily the moonbeams fall,
And through the windows of the keep
In gleams of light, where 'neath the steep
The shadows of the castle sleep
    Upon the dark lake's breast ;
But quickly now a change has past,
And o'er the clear moon gathering fast,
Clouds in threatening masses rise,
And soon her brightness fades and dies,
And on the lake and o'er the skies
    The night's broad shadows rest.
" Hurrah for the yacht, bring out the bottle,
With something stiff I must wet my throttle,"
The Abbot cried, as up he sprung
In garments moist that round him clung :
    " To-night of water I've had enough,

So now I'll mix some stronger stuff.
Come on, my boys, let us be jolly,
And away with melancholy;
Here's to the Templars, those 'monks of the screw,'
I doubt not that they were a jovial crew,
Their vows they kept in a general way,
And broke them but every other day.
They swore to abstain from women and wine,
And on the plainest food to dine;
Yet these same Templars would not shun
A promising spree or a bit of fun:
They loved the glance of a woman's eye,
And even from kisses would not fly,
Although the canon sternly chid,[1]
And all such naughty things forbid.
They loved on rich ragouts to dine,
And took like gentlemen their wine,
And then they fought like thorough bricks,
And made the Pagans cut their sticks.
Then hip! hurrah! for the Templars bold,
And hip! hurrah! for their ruined hold,
Hip! hurrah! and one cheer more—"
When down upon the cabin floor
The Abbot falls, and in his sleep
Dreams of Urquhart's ruined keep.

On leaving our anchorage we had at first a gentle breeze from the right quarter, but this soon died almost away, and after a tedious voyage we came to at a little distance from the mouth of the Foyers. We landed at a small wooden jetty, and after a pleasant walk through birch woods, reached

---

[1] See the Canon *De osculis fugiendis*.

the lower and principal fall, where the stream, by
a single leap of seventy feet, precipitates itself
from a ledge of rock into the black caldron beneath.
The river was much swollen by rains, and on the
projecting point where we stood we were almost
deafened by the roar of the fall, and blinded by
the whirling spray. The Fall of Foyers is generally
supposed to be the highest in Scotland; but this is
a great mistake. The Falls of Glomack, on the
stream that runs into the head of Loch Ling, on
the coast of Ross-shire, are three times as high;
nor can a greater contrast be imagined than that
presented by these two falls. At Foyers, though
there are lofty and rugged rocks frowning over a
deep chasm, there is also much verdure and beauty
in the waving woods and the rocks tufted by grass
and ferns. At the Glomack, on the other hand,
there is neither tree, shrub, grass, nor fern; all is
desolation where the wild waters fling themselves
over "the herbless granite." The Upper Fall of
Foyers is only thirty feet in height, and is half a
mile farther up the stream. A bridge spans the
torrent just below the fall, and was some years ago
the scene of a frightful catastrophe. The horses in
the carriage of a Mr. Rose, of Inverness, took
fright, and dragged the vehicle, containing himself

and his two daughters, over the parapet of the
bridge into the rocky bed of the stream below.
One of the ladies was killed, and Mr. Rose and the
other severely injured. To us it seemed a miracle
that any of them should have escaped drowning or
being dashed to pieces.

We cast anchor for the night on the west side
of the bay, near the entrance to Glen Moriston.
The shores of the lake between that glen and Glen
Urquhart are very picturesque, adorned with
natural wood, with gray crags here and there
breaking through. Between these two valleys
rises the lofty summit of Mealfourvonie, the
highest mountain in sight. During the day we
tried the lead whilst lying becalmed, but found no
bottom with 110 fathoms. We spent a Sunday
at Glen Moriston, which was what Sam Slick calls
"a juicy day in the country." The rain poured
incessantly, and thick gray mists obscured the
whole of the glen. There are, near its opening, a
fine waterfall and a bridge and sawmill, which
form an admirable subject for the sketcher.

On leaving Loch Ness we had a pleasant sail
through Loch Oich, passing the noble ruins of
Invergarry Castle. The mountain-slopes on the
banks of Loch Oich are covered with the most

beautiful verdure from their summits to the very
water's edge, and along the shores of Loch Lochy
the pasture is also very luxuriant. There is a
beautiful bay and good anchorage at its south-
western extremity; and two miles inland, separated
by a lovely wooded valley, lies Loch Arkaig. At
one point, the narrow path along this glen is, for a
considerable distance, quite overshadowed by trees,
whose branches meet overhead, and hence it is
poetically termed by the Highlanders "the dark
mile of Arkaig." The shores of Loch Arkaig are in
places densely wooded, and its surface is diversified
by islands, but on the whole the scenery around it
is tame.

After leaving Loch Lochy we had a pleasant
passage along the canal and through the eight
locks which form "Neptune's Staircase," and came
to for the night near the sea lock leading down to
Loch Eil. The dues through the Caledonian Canal
are very moderate; we paid only thirty shillings;
and for one shilling were furnished, at the entrance,
with a chart of the canal, which we found most
useful in pointing out the best anchorages.

In spite of the threatening aspect of the clouds,
which lay piled up in heavy masses along the sides
of Glen Nevis, two of us started to visit and sketch

the old Castle of Inverlochy, about a couple of
miles distant from where we lay ; but we had
scarcely begun our sketches when a thunderstorm
burst over us, and, leaving them unfinished, we
were glad to hurry back, getting drenched through
long before we reached the welcome shelter of our
cabins. A beautiful morning dawned upon us
after a stormy night, and by ten o'clock we had
accomplished the passage through the sea lock, and
were at anchor near the quay at Fort-William.

As the weather was beautiful, our first care
upon landing was to proceed to the Caledonian
Hotel, the principal inn at Fort-William, and make
arrangements for the ascent of Ben Nevis. These
were soon effected ; sandwiches were cut, whisky-
flasks filled, and we were just preparing for a start,
when two gentlemen staying at the inn requested
to be allowed to join our party. One was a young
Dutchman, and the other a mercantile gentleman
from the good town of Glasgow. Both were
attired in black hats and trousers, and wore
Wellington boots with thin soles. The Dutchman
had never ascended a mountain in his life, his
severest experience in climbing having been the
ascent of the six hundred steps that lead to the
highest platform on the spire of Antwerp Cathe-

dral. However, though in both their cases the flesh was weak, yet the spirit was willing, and they subsequently displayed the greatest pluck and perseverance, in spite of their unsuitable dress and the excessive fatigue from which they suffered. In those days there was no royal road to the top of Ben Nevis, no Observatory, and no hotel, and the climb was a long and very steep one. The writer has been at the top of forty-seven mountains in Scotland over 3000 feet high, but none of them were much steeper than Ben Nevis was. The charge for the services of a guide is ten shillings, whether one only or a party of tourists ascend the mountain. Our guide was named Alexander Macrae, an ill-put-together, queer-looking Celt, but a capital walker, and quite a character, as, indeed, might easily have been divined from the roguish twinkle of his quick black eyes. The height of Ben Nevis above the sea is 4406 feet, *all* requiring to be ascended, as, unlike the generality of the Scotch and Swiss mountains, which rise from elevated plateaux, it rises at once from the sea-level. It is five miles from Fort-William to the summit, measured in a straight line, and from three to four hours are generally required to accomplish the distance. For more than a mile we proceeded

along a level road, passing on our left the fort
which gives its name to the town. On our right
was the entrance to the beautiful Glen Nevis, and
between us and the Lochy lay the ruins of the fine
old Castle of Inverlochy, and at a little distance
beyond it the Ben Nevis distillery, one of the most
celebrated in Scotland, which for many years
belonged to a man known throughout the Highlands as "Long John." We commenced the
ascent by a very stiff pull up a grassy spur of
the mountain, which slopes steeply upwards to a
height of about 1200 feet. Many were the
halts of our mercantile comrades, loud their complaints, and frequent their applications to the
whisky-flasks, ere we gained the summit, and it
required the greatest persuasion and encouragement
to induce them to proceed; the Dutchman declar-
ing that hills were not made for him, and that
nothing would lead any of his countrymen to
attempt such an exertion, did they only know the
toil that awaited them.

On surmounting this shoulder of the mountain
we came to a comparatively level moss, crossed it,
slanted along the corner of another offshoot of
Ben Nevis, and then found ourselves on the banks
of a dark mountain tarn, formed by the drainage

from the steep sides of the hollow which it fills.
Near this we came to a halt, before attempting the
remainder of the ascent. The guide drank like
a fish and smoked like a steam-engine, and in both
these respects our companions imitated him. The
day was charming, and the view already most
interesting and extensive. After a short rest we
again started, rousing our companions with considerable difficulty, who appreciated cold grog and
cigars much better than climbing. We then
commenced the most fatiguing part of our journey
—over a perfect wilderness of loose stones of all
sizes, utterly destitute of every trace of vegetation.
These soon told upon the Wellington boots of
our friends, and the Glasgow man at last lay down
and fell fast asleep, and, on being aroused, was
only induced to proceed by the appalling stories
which our waggish guide invented and related
for his benefit, of the mishaps of various tourists
who had yielded to fatigue and fallen asleep during
the ascent. From this point, however, he and the
Dutchman alternately lagged behind and shot
ahead of each other; but both compelled the
guide and ourselves to make frequent halts, till
at length, about a mile from the top, observing
some clouds drifting up from the southward, and

fearful lest the view from the summit should become obscured, we started forward, telling the guide to remain behind and bring up the stragglers. Shortly before this we had made a second prolonged halt at a spot called "The Well," where a spring of most delicious water gushes out from the stones. This "diamond in the desert" is about 3000 feet above Fort-William.

Soon after leaving our companions we came upon a square patch of snow of considerable extent, and apparently of some depth, and, a little beyond it, caught sight of the stone cairn erected to mark the summit. Advancing towards it, we skirted the edge of a tremendous precipice, which goes sheer down 1700 feet into the dark glen below. The summit of Ben Nevis is an almost level surface, totally destitute of water and vegetation, and composed entirely of shattered fragments of stone. Close to the verge of the precipice, and on the highest point of the mountain, stands the huge cairn erected by the Trigonometrical Survey ; we clambered to the top of it, and stood on the loftiest summit in Great Britain, 110 feet higher than Ben Macdhui, which for a long time disputed the palm with Ben Nevis. The view all around was magnificent ; for months there had not been a clearer day on the top. To the northward we saw the sharp peak of Fannich, in Ross-shire, the serrated points of the Coolins, the fine mountain mass of Rum, part of Eigg, the Island of Mull, and the nearer land of Lismore. Southward lay Ben Cruachan, Ben Ima, Ben Lomond, Ben More, Ben Lawers, and Schichallion. To the eastward the huge mass of the Cairngorm mountains and Ben Wyvis were distinctly visible; whilst, farther off, a silver line showed the distant waters of the Moray Firth. We saw both the eastern and western seas. Nearer were the white-topped stony peaks at the head of Glen Nevis, the sharp red points of the mountains above Glencoe, and those between that glen and the head of Loch Etive. At our feet lay Lochaber, marked by the gleam of its small blue lakes, Inverlochy Castle, Neptune's Staircase, Corpach, or the field of dead bodies, and the beautiful expanse of Loch Eil, at the head of which Prince Charles for the last time met the clans.

Half an hour after we had reached the summit, we saw the guide approaching with our companions, both of whom, especially the Dutchman, we heartily congratulated on having at length reached the top in spite of fatigue and difficulties. We observed the Dutchman writing the name of *la dame de ses pensées* upon one of his calling-cards, and then dropping it into a hole near the top of the cairn, where, the guide assured us, lay the cards of some hundred tourists, who had thus "ticketed" Ben Nevis. Our friend also chipped off a fragment of stone to carry back to Holland as a *souvenir* of the hardest day's work he had ever undergone. After a lengthened stay on the summit and a glance into the precipitous chasm which opened on one side of us, and into Glen Nevis on the other, near the head of which streams down a slender thread of silver over a precipice 400 feet high, we commenced our descent, the burden of which might well have been "rattle his bones over the stones." The roughness of the road soon told on our companions. The Glasgowegian several times lay down and fell asleep, and the Dutchman declared that £500 would not tempt him again to ascend Ben Nevis.

By way of varying the route, we proposed to the guide to descend into Glen Nevis, wade across the stream, and return to Fort-William by the level road that runs alongside of it. This he at once agreed to, at the same time warning us that the descent would be very steep and rapid.

About half-way down to the glen the stones ceased,
and were succeeded by a steep slippery slope of
verdant pasturage. Here we left our comrades in
charge of the guide and of a handsome little
Highland gillie, who had carried their coats for
them, and had crossed all the stones on his bare
feet, which were a good deal cut and blistered.
We then descended at a rattling pace, passing
through quantities of high ferns near the bottom,
gained the valley, waded across the stream, and
sat down on its grassy banks to await the arrival
of our friends and their tail. It was amusing
to watch them, some 1500 feet above us,
toiling slowly and cautiously along, and the guide
attempting to persuade them to adopt a more
rapid mode of locomotion by sitting down and
sliding along the slope. Of this he gave them
a practical illustration, which the Dutchman
attempted to follow, but apparently soon found
that black cloth trousers were but an imperfect
protection against the friction produced by contact
with the steep sides of Ben Nevis, for he speedily
resumed the perpendicular, and at length, after
many a slip and stumble, succeeded in reaching
the banks of the Nevis, followed at a considerable
distance by his Glasgow friend. There he lay

down on his back on the stony banks of the
stream, and, holding up his Wellington-clad extremities, entreated the guide to pull off his boots,
which that worthy at last accomplished by dint
of desperate tugging, which drew forth the most
ludicrous contortions and exclamations from the
unfortunate Dutchman, who then rose and staggered
towards the stream, which, though shallow, ran
with considerable rapidity. In the middle of the
water he lost his balance, and, by way of steadying
himself, thrust one arm to the bottom of the
stream, and got himself wetted up to the shoulder.
At length he reached the bank where we were
sitting, and laid himself down at full length on
the grass, dead beat. His friend now made his
appearance on the farther bank, and the gillie
performed the same kind office for him that the
guide had for the Dutchman. Apparently, his
Wellingtons were less obstinate, but when he
arrived at our side of the river he was scarcely in
better condition than his foreign friend. After
some time allowed them to recover, our guide
insisted on proceeding; and once on a smooth
and level road they got on famously, having really
shown during the whole expedition great perseverance, pluck, and good-nature. They were badly

dressed, unaccustomed to walking, and drank and smoked too much, so that their exhausted condition on our arrival at Fort-William was scarcely to be wondered at. We returned to the yacht about six o'clock, well appetised, but quite free from fatigue. We found that our worthy sailing-master had met with an old acquaintance at Fort-William, had spent the day with him, and had returned on board in a state of perfect happiness and considerable inebriation, which produced a curious effect upon his somewhat saturnine temperament. He was overpoweringly kind and attentive, smiling at everything and everybody, to the intense delight and amusement of the crew.

We set sail from Fort-William early next morning, bound for Ballachulish, in Loch Leven. The wind was unfavourable, and we had a dead beat to windward almost the whole way. At Corran Ferry, where the loch is only a quarter of a mile wide, the tide ran very strongly, the water all around us boiling and seething in eddies and whirlpools. Fortunately we had the ebb with us, and got through easily enough. During the day we sailed past the entrance of several beautiful glens, particularly Inverscaddle and Ardgour. Considerable care is required in entering Loch

Leven, as, on one side, a long sandy spit runs out
for a great distance, and on this the water is very
shallow, but its extremity is marked by a red
buoy. After rounding this we had to beat up
through the Narrows, where, owing to the light
and baffling wind, and tide against us, we ran
aground, but luckily got off without any damage.
In the afternoon we came to anchor close to the
entrance of Glencoe, and not far from the Ballachulish slate quarries, the *débris* from which, constantly thrown into the loch, has now formed an
excellent harbour, where large vessels may lie
afloat at all times of the tide. Near us were two
or three small green islands, one of which has for
centuries been used as a burial-ground by the
Macdonalds of Glencoe and Lochaber. We lost no
time in landing and setting out for Glencoe; but
we had only got a little distance beyond the old
ruined house which was the scene of the massacre
which has made the memory of King William
infamous, when we were forced to beat a retreat
by the rain, which poured down in torrents.

On getting back to the yacht we turned in at
an early hour, contemplating an early start next
morning; but we were not destined to enjoy unbroken slumbers, for, a little after midnight, we

were all aroused by a tremendous row proceeding
from the cabin where our worthy skipper was
enjoying the sweets of repose and sleeping off his
debauch at Fort-William. We found the ancient
mariner yelling like a maniac, and twisting and

THE ENTRANCE TO GLENCOE.

writhing about as if in the last agony. In fact,
he was struggling with the nightmare, and appeared to have decidedly the worst of the contest.

Next morning was gray and cloudy, with
drizzling rain, and the glen filled with drifting
mist, curling in wreaths along the sides of the
mountains. Notwithstanding which, armed with
umbrellas, waterproofs, and whisky-flasks, we

started to explore the far-famed beauties of
Glencoe. Where it opens upon Loch Leven the
glen is wide, green, and fertile, and the brawling
stream of Cona winds along an almost level valley;
but, about two miles from the opening, it makes
an abrupt turn to the left, and its character all at
once assumes an aspect of rugged grandeur. On
one side is the huge conical mass of Meall Mor,
with its almost perpendicular sides; near its
summit yawns a lofty dark fissure, in an inaccessible position, which tradition has named the Cave
of Fingal, who must have been a first-rate crags-
man, and not at all nice in his choice of a lodging.
At the base of Meall Mor lies a small dark lake,
while on the opposite side of the glen rise sharp
serrated summits, very similar to the peaks of
Glens Sannox and Sligachan. Innumerable rills
were rushing down the scarred and furrowed sides
of the mountains, every gully forming a watercourse; whilst the stream of Cona, swollen by the
rains, and every moment increasing in volume,
swept foaming and fretting along its narrow
channel.

Not far from the head of the valley stands a
bridge, by which the road crosses a small rivulet,
and from this point one of the finest views of the

glen may be obtained. Whilst standing on this bridge and looking across to the opposite side of the valley, we observed at a considerable elevation, and near the head of a narrow watercourse, a deep circular hollow or corrie, with a mass of huge stone blocks piled in irregular heaps right across its opening. This appeared to us to have all the appearance of the terminal moraine of an ancient glacier. On our return, soon after we had passed the small lake of Triochtan, a beautiful effect of sunshine became visible in the glen: a brilliant rainbow spanned it from side to side, its whole dimensions being entirely within the valley, and the most exquisite prismatic hues were reflected upon the grass at the bottom of the glen, and upon the dark rocky masses along its sides.

Before leaving Loch Leven we paid a visit to the slate quarries of Ballachulish, which give employment to several hundred hands. They do not seem to be worked with much energy, as we found fifteen vessels waiting for cargoes, some of them having been detained for months. The slates are inferior in quality to the Welsh, but more durable and cheaper. There is seldom a great stock on hand, and they take about three weeks to load a vessel of one hundred tons. Loch

Leven extends about seven miles above the entrance to Glencoe — deep, narrow, river-like — hemmed in by dark mountains with promontories and wooded knolls projecting boldly into the loch, and beautifully diversifying the character of its shores. Upon the whole, we are inclined to consider Loch Leven as one of the finest of our Scottish sea-lochs. It lies in the midst of beauties of the most varied and enchanting description : there are green islands, green wooded slopes, clumps of trees, with the blue smoke of cottages curling up from amongst the foliage, as well as dark glens and stern and sterile mountains. There is no weak point about the scenery ; it is " of beauty all compact."

Bidding farewell to Loch Leven with regret, we set sail for Oban. The wind was from the northward, which here requires to be carefully watched. We met with heavy squalls whilst passing the high land of Morven, opposite the island of Lismore, and off the mouth of Loch Achray. We had to take in our topsail, double-reef the mainsail, and shift jibs, and even then had quite enough of it in the squalls. During the process of shifting jibs and reefing, our largest boat broke adrift, the skipper himself having made

her fast with, what the event proved to be, but
a "slippery hitch." Before we observed her, she
had drifted a long way to leeward, and was fast
approaching the rocky beach of Lismore, where
she would soon have gone to pieces. About was
the word, and we tacked in pursuit of her; twice
we got alongside, and twice failed in securing her.
The third time we got a grapnel from below, hove
it aboard, and at last succeeded, at the expense
of some damage to her thwarts, in again securing
and making her fast. About four o'clock we
reached Oban, and came to anchor in its safe and
beautiful bay.

We lost no time in pulling on shore, in order
to lay in stores and to visit the ruins of the old
Castle of Dunstaffnage (castle of two islands),
situated on a peninsula near the entrance of Loch
Etive, and three miles distant from Oban. Part
of the structure is of unknown antiquity, and the
ruins consist of four massive walls united at the
angles by round towers. The view from the top
of the castle, which is still accessible, is very
extensive, embracing Loch Etive, Lochnell, the
mountains of Morven and Appin, and the green
mound which is supposed to mark the site of
Beregonium, the ancient capital of the Picts.

The Irish Scoti, or Dalriadic Scots, colonised, and for three hundred years occupied, this part of the Highlands, and Dunstaffnage is supposed to have been their principal stronghold.

The next was a pet day — warm, calm, and bright—made for enjoyment and out-of-door existence. We spent the forenoon in wandering about the grounds, and in visiting the beautiful castle of Dunollie, thus graphically described by Sir Walter Scott: "Nothing can be more wildly beautiful than the situation of Dunollie. The ruins are situated upon a bold and precipitous promontory overhanging Loch Etive, and distant about a mile from the village and port of Oban. The principal part which remains is the donjon or keep; but fragments of other buildings, over-grown with ivy, attest that it had been once a place of importance, as large, probably, as Ardtornish or Dunstaffnage. These fragments enclose a courtyard, of which the keep probably formed one side, the entrance being by a steep ascent from the neck of the isthmus, formerly cut across by a moat, and defended doubtless by outworks and a drawbridge. Beneath the castle stands the present mansion of the family. A huge upright pillar or detached fragment of that sort of rock called plum-pudding stone, upon the shore, about a quarter of a mile from the castle, is called Clach-na-can, or the Dog's Pillar, because Fingal is said to have used it as a stake to which he bound his celebrated dog Bran."

In the evening we rowed to the south side of the bay, and afterwards ascended a low hill, from which, for a very small amount of trouble, a magnificent view may be obtained. This evening, in the light of a glorious sunset, every object was clearly defined : the bay and town of Oban, the castled crag of Dunollie, the green islands of Kerrera and Lismore, Morven, Appin, the Sound of Mull overshadowed by the lofty Ben More, and, in the opposite direction, the twin peaks of Ben Cruachan, and the huge mountains beyond, near the head of Loch Etive. The tints of some of the distant mountains were exquisitely beautiful, partly a rich purple, and partly a deep slate-gray, contrasting strongly with the gorgeous orange and golden hues around the setting sun.

It was a fine but cold morning when we left Oban, bound for the Firth of Clyde. We made a rapid run along the Sound of Kerrera, through the Slate islands, past Scarba and the entrances to Loch Crinan and Loch Melford, and thence

into the strait between the Island of Jura and
the Mull of Cantire. We passed the whirlpool of
Corryvreckan on our starboard hand, but, owing
to the state of the tide, there were but few indi-
cations of its existence. The wind, which had
gradually been freshening ever since the morning,
now increased to a gale. Fortunately it was a
land wind, and there was little sea, but we had
to strike our topmast, and double-reef the mainsail, and, even then, were carrying a plank of
the deck under water. We passed several vessels
running up the Sound for shelter under easy sail,
and, as it would have been folly to attempt to
round the Mull of Cantire in such weather, we
determined to follow their example, and accordingly put about and ran for Loch Swin, a noble
arm of the sea, which for ten miles indents the
Mull of Cantire, forming a safe and spacious
anchorage, with a clear entrance, and a depth
varying from three to thirteen fathoms. We
anchored a mile above Castle Swin, which occupies
a commanding position on a projecting rock.
Where we lay the water was smooth, yet it blew
so hard all day that we were obliged to have two
anchors out to prevent dragging. Next morning
the gale had moderated, though it still blew

freshly, and gray watery clouds were drifting along the hills. As the day wore on, however, the weather improved, and we were able to land and visit Castle Swin, which gives its name to the loch, and is believed to have been built by Sweno, King of Denmark. It forms an interesting memorial of those days when every bay and loch along our coasts was exposed to the incursions of Danish pirates, and when the kings of Norway not only possessed a large part of the Highlands and Islands, but even threatened the independence of the kingdom of Scotland. The people in the cottages near the castle assured us that it was twelve hundred years old—a degree of antiquity which we were inclined to consider very questionable. It is a magnificent old ruin, as large as Dunstaffnage, square in its general shape, but with a tall round tower projecting at one of the angles. We found the great court occupied by a patch of corn, the basement of the round tower turned into a kitchen-garden, and an inner court choked up by a rank growth of hemlock and nettles; yet the proprietor is a man of immense fortune, a fraction of which might surely be spent in keeping this interesting old ruin in tolerable order: at present it suffers from the most utter neglect.

Next morning we made a very early start, succeeded in rounding the Mull of Cantire, of stormy fame, without encountering anything like rough weather, had a fine run up the beautiful Firth of Clyde, and finished a delightful month's cruise by dropping our anchor in the calm waters of Gourock Bay.

CASTLE URQUHART, CALEDONIAN CANAL.

HEAD OF LOCH ETIVE.

CHAPTER III

CRUISE TO THE HEAD OF LOCH ETIVE

AMONG the many arms of the sea which indent the western coast of Scotland between the Mull of Cantire and Cape Wrath, there is none that will better reward the adventurous yachtsman than Loch Etive, which stretches from its entrance, marked out by the noble ruins of Dunstaffnage Castle, first in an easterly, and then in a northeasterly direction, for more than twenty miles, and affords in the course of that extent a remarkable variety of grand and beautiful scenery. There are wooded headlands, winding bays, and valleys full of cultivated beauty, as well as frowning rocks, and lofty mountains with scarred and rugged sides, opening into deep corries,—the favourite haunts of the red-deer. In some places the gently-sloping shores let in the sunshine upon the broad bosom of the lake, while in others vast mountains cast an almost perpetual shadow over its narrow waters. The lower loch, between Dunstaffnage and Bunawe, forms a striking contrast to the upper, between Bunawe and Glen Etive ; the former, picturesque and sylvan, with low rounded hills, undulating promontories, sequestered with fertile valleys, excites only pleasing emotions ; the latter, dark and narrow, with precipitous shores given up to the sheep and the red-deer, arouses feelings of awe and admiration ; while both united combine to form a whole which cannot be surpassed by any other sea-loch in Great Britain.

At its entrance, a short distance above Dun-staffnage, are the dangerous rapids of Connel Ferry, where the tide runs more than eight miles an hour, and, at ebb, breaks right across the narrow and rocky channel in one sheet of white foam ; while, to add to the risk, a rock, covered at high water, shoots up almost in the centre of the passage. It is therefore advisable for those yachtsmen who wish to explore Loch Etive to secure the services of a pilot at Oban, in order to guard against the dangers and difficulties of its navigation.

The best winds for ascending Loch Etive are south or south-westerly, the most favourable for descending north-easterly. The Narrows must be passed with a leading wind and the first of flood ascending, and with slack water flood or the first of ebb in descending.

Having made these preliminary remarks with regard to a loch, of whose very existence some of our readers may possibly be ignorant, we shall now proceed to the narrative of our cruise. At eleven o'clock on a fine July morning we sailed from Oban Bay in a cutter yacht of twelve tons, passing between the ivy-clad keep of Dunollie Castle, the ancient seat of the MacDougalls of Lorn, and the Maiden Isle, shaving the latter as close as possible in order to keep the deep-water channel. The tides at Connel, though only four miles distant, are two hours later than at Oban; and when a vessel arrives too soon, or when the wind is unfavourable for passing the Rapids, she ought to anchor in the bay on the south side of Dunstaffnage Castle, where she will be perfectly sheltered, and may wait for a suitable wind and tide. The channel between Dunstaffnage and the larger of the two islands from

H

which it takes its name is in some places very
shallow ; but, by keeping near the centre, and
somewhat closer to the island than the castle, all
danger will be avoided. There is no passage between the two islands, but there is a practicable
channel on the northern side of the little isle.
The view of the entrance to Loch Etive, shortly
before arriving at Dunstaffnage, is exceedingly
picturesque, and the sketcher would do well to
draw it from this point ; the grand old castle forms
an admirable foreground, the contours of the deep
Bay of Lochnell, with its wooded heights and
silvery beach, are full of grace and variety, while
the distance is nobly filled up by Ben Durinish
and the twin peaks of the lofty Ben Cruachan. In
Lochnell Bay we observed the ruins of the castle of
the same name accidentally burnt down some years
ago, and the green mound which is supposed to
mark the site of Beregonium, the ancient capital of
the Picts.

After passing Dunstaffnage we shaped our
course for Connel,[1] keeping the point of the larger

---

[1] Connel is thus alluded to by Sir Walter Scott in the 1st Canto of the
Lord of the Isles :-

> From where Mingarry, sternly placed,
> O'erawes the woodland and the waste,
> To where Dunstaffnage hears the raging
> Of Connel with his rocks engaging.

island and the ferry-house in a line, passed the
long gravelly spit of Lidiack Point, and shortly
afterwards the Rapids; where, as we had nicely
calculated our time, and had a favourable breeze,
we encountered neither difficulty nor danger.   In
passing, we kept the rock in the centre of the
Narrows on our port hand, which is the best plan,
though there is also a clear channel on the other
side of it.   The ferry at Connel, narrow in itself, is
still further contracted by a reef of rocks which
runs partly across it, and the roaring of this great
salt-water cataract, during ebb tide, may often be
heard ten miles off, though the fall is only about
six feet.   Owing to this inequality of the waters
without and within, there is seven hours' flood and
five hours' ebb at Connel; and it takes two hours
for the tide without to equalise the waters pressing
down from within.   Soon after getting through
the Narrows we passed the beautifully - situated
mansion house of Ardchattan, standing amidst
thick woods and fertile fields.   Near it are the
ruins of the ancient priory of the same name, built
by John MacDougall in the thirteenth century, and
where Robert the Bruce once held a parliament.
It was burnt by Colkitto during the wars of
Montrose.   The next point of interest was the

village of Bunawe, about twelve miles from Oban, where Loch Etive receives its principal feeder, the river Awe, which issues from the side of the lake of the same name, and traverses the romantic pass of Brander on the flanks of Ben Cruachan, the scene of the defeat of John of Lorn by Robert the Bruce.

At Bunawe the bolder features of the scenery around Loch Etive begin to develop themselves; between it and Glen Etive there is no road, and the pedestrian must be content to scramble along mountain - sides, cross gullies and watercourses, wind round bays, and wade through bogs, before he can reach the head of the upper loch; and even then he will have fifteen miles farther to walk before he gains Kingshouse, the nearest inn, a day's work sufficient to knock up any but the stoutest mountaineer. Above Bunawe the dangers of the navigation of the loch, with the exception of those arising from sudden squalls, may be said to be over; there are no rocks or shoals, and, on both sides, there is deep water to within a cable's length of the shore. The huge base of Cruachan on one side, and the copse-clad crags of Ben Durinish on the other, confine its waters; and farther up, Cruachan is succeeded by Ben Starav, opposed by

the dark buttresses of Ben Trilleachan; while at
the head of the lake rise the sharp peaks of the
three Buchails, the giant watchers of Glen Etive.
On the sides of Cruachan open up the wild Glen Noe
and the green and smiling Glen Kinglass, a beautiful pastoral valley watered by the Armaddie river,
in which the fishing is first-rate, but most strictly
preserved.   The whole of the district around Little
or Upper Loch Etive forms the Marquis of Bread-
albane's deer forest; his shooting-lodge is situated
some distance up Glen Kinglass; red-deer and
gamekeepers are the lords of the mountains and
streams, and any attempt to cast a fly either in
the Etive or Kinglass will at once be stopped.

Loch Ness generally enjoys the reputation of
being the deepest lake in Scotland, but our
Highland Palinurus assured us that this was a
popular error, and asserted the superior claims of
Loch Etive.   There had been, he said, a tradition
of long standing that, near Strono (as a bluff
projecting boldly into the lake is called), its waters
were fathomless, and this he, and some Oban
fishermen, determined a few years ago to test.
They accordingly procured 230 fathoms of line,
fastened an anchor to the end of it, commenced
sounding, and found the greatest depth off Strono

to be 206 fathoms, or some hundred feet deeper than the deepest part of Loch Ness. In reality there is a considerable depression here, but only to the extent of about 200 feet.

When about five miles from the head of the loch, and seven above Bunawe, the wind, which had all day been light and baffling, at last headed us, and we therefore anchored for the night close to the shore, a little below the granite quarries of Barr. There was a quantity of natural birch-wood all along the sloping banks above our anchorage, among which charcoal-burners were busily engaged in preparing charcoal for the use of the iron furnaces at Bunawe; and wreaths of blue smoke were curling up through the light green foliage, marking where the heaps were smouldering, carefully watched day and night to prevent their setting fire to the surrounding trees. Loch Etive is very subject to sudden and violent squalls of wind from the high lands around, which require to be carefully guarded against. We were not, however, disturbed in our somewhat exposed anchorage, the rain which poured incessantly during the whole night being sufficient to damp the spirits of the most boisterous squall that ever roared across a Highland loch.

Early next morning we got under weigh, and

with a favourable breeze made sail for the head
of the loch. After passing the granite quarries
we entered upon the wildest and most rugged
part of the scenery, a narrow reach of dark water
blackened by the long shadows of Ben Starav and
Ben Trilleachan. As the mists gradually cleared
away from the mountain-sides and summits, we
saw the effects of the heavy rains which had for
some days been falling. Every gully and rift on
the precipitous hill-sides was swept by a torrent
pouring down in white foam, and the air was filled
with the hollow sound of innumerable waterfalls ;
the weather too was in admirable keeping with
the stern character of the landscape around us ;
wreaths of gray mist were drifting along the
mountain - sides, now hiding their sharp peaks
and deep ravines, and now floating aside and
revealing them, while occasional gleams of sunshine gilded the rocks above us, and lighted up
the sullen waters of the loch. The sides of Ben
Starav bear deep scars of the ravages of the
winter torrents, which have in many places torn
up the soil to a great breadth, and replaced it
by a perfect chaos of stones and *débris*. On the
opposite side, the vast mass of Ben Trilleachan
rises almost perpendicularly, presenting a suc-

cession of huge rocky buttresses towering up like
the walls of some castle of Titans. Many of the
crags are broken into singular and fantastic forms,
and would afford Mr. Ruskin most curious ex-
amples of "rock-fracture." There is a striking
resemblance between this mountain and the hill
of Meall Mor which rises above Loch Triochtan
in Glencoe; indeed the mountains around this
upper reach of Loch Etive are very similar to
those of Glencoe, which, however, cannot, in like
manner, boast of a fine arm of the sea winding
among their recesses. The distance between the
two glens is not great, and there is a mountain
pass near the head of Loch Etive well worth
exploring, which after about three hours' rough
walking will lead the pedestrian into Glencoe.

The river Etive runs into the head of the
loch through the glen of the same name; it is
an excellent fishing stream, but, like all those in
this neighbourhood, strictly preserved. Although,
however, river-fishing is prohibited, there is capital
fishing for whiting in Upper Loch Etive, and
those yachtsmen who are fond of it would do
well to provide themselves with a store of bait
from the mussel-bank off Bunawe. It is no uncommon thing—at least so we were told—for a

party of four fishermen (each working two hand-
lines) to catch from two thousand to four thousand
whitings in a single day. Besides whitings there
are other fish, denizens of Loch Etive, of a less
attractive character, namely conger eels, which
(according to our pilot) grow to between seven
and eight feet long, and are almost as carnivorous
as sharks; indeed he tried to prevent us from
bathing at Bunawe in case we should become
food for eels.

After remaining some hours at the head of
the loch and walking a short distance up Glen
Etive, dominated by its three Buchails, we re-
traced our steps to the yacht, and at two o'clock
set out on our return voyage. The wind unfortunately was southerly, and we had the tide
against us, so that we had to beat down the
whole way, and were at last obliged about seven
o'clock to come to anchor, a cable's length from
the shore, in a beautiful little bay just above
the embouchure of the river Awe. There is a
store at Bunawe for the use of the workmen
engaged in the granite quarries and foundry, at
which biscuits, grocery, and occasionally butcher's
meat may be procured ; but the yachtsmen exploring Loch Etive ought not to trust to this,

but should provide themselves with stores at
Oban ; for as the Narrows at Connel can only
be passed either way with a leading wind, they
may possibly be detained several days within
the loch. Above Bunawe nothing can be got ;
and at the farmhouses below, the eggs, butter,
and milk are all bespoke by the public coaches
which pass daily, so that they do not find it
worth their while to sell anything to such birds
of passage as yachtsmen. There is a fine view,
looking up the loch from the spot where we
lay, taking in Ben Starav and the glens between
it and Cruachan, while the copse-clad crags of
Ben Durinish come well in in the foreground; we
sketched the scene, and would beg to recommend
it to our brother amateurs.

Next morning was bright and warm with a
light breeze, so we got early under weigh, and
passed safely the dangerous bank off the mouth of
the Awe which is *not* laid down in the charts.
Keep it on the port hand going down, but do
not shave the opposite shore too closely, as there
are large stones off it; below this the loch is
deep and spacious. In the afternoon the wind
failed us, and we were obliged to give up all
hopes of getting through Connel until the follow-

ing day. We therefore anchored in Stonefield
Bay, between the south shore and Macnab's Island,
marked by a few plane trees and some traces of
ruined buildings. This anchorage is more out of
the tides than any other in Loch Etive. There
was a glorious sunset ; the sun, sinking behind
the Sound of Mull, threw a bright column of
golden flame across the quiet bay where we were
moored, and the near hills in deep purple shadow
brought out the warm tones of the sunset, while
the eastern sky was of the deepest azure and
without a cloud.

To-day our invaluable pilot—who is evidently
impressed with the idea that we have not an
adequate conception of the dangers of Connel
Ferry, a place which, he told us, he never passed
" without every hair of his head standing on
end "—has been amusing us by relating appalling
stories of the dangers of descending, which, he
will have it, is much more hazardous than ascending Connel. Three vessels, according to his story,
are at this moment grating their ribs on the
rocks at the bottom of the Narrows, having
attempted to pass them at an improper time ;
in one of these were two brothers ; their sloop
struck upon the rock in the centre of the channel ;

one tried to escape in the boat which was instantly
swamped, and the other, while attempting to let
go an anchor, was washed overboard and drowned.
In the other two cases the vessels perished, but
the crews were saved. He also told us that he
remembered of twenty-three lives having been
lost upon Loch Etive, chiefly from the overset-
ting of boats in the violent gusts that rush down
from the mountains; and (awful to relate) none
of the bodies were ever found, having fallen a
prey to the carnivorous congers which infest the
loch. The worthy pilot, however, draws a very
long bow in everything that relates to the
Highlands, and his stories require a large grain
of salt to be swallowed along with them.

According to him the crops in some places
on the wild shores of Loch Etive are as early
as in the Lothians; the Hebrides are as fertile
as the Isle of Wight; and the cliffs of Staffa
higher than those of the Giant's Causeway. His
stories, however, of the difficulty and danger of
descending Connel Ferry had their effect, and
we began to be troubled with uneasy visions of a
fortnight's detention in Loch Etive, of supplies
running short, and of being reduced to eat the
boy without pickles. These somewhat interfered

with our tranquillity, though moored for the
night in as quiet an anchorage as ever received
a wearied sailor. Fortunately these presentiments
of evil were soon dispelled, for next morning
we started at six o'clock, passed Little Connel,
where we were a good deal tossed about in the
tide race, reached the Rapids just at the slack
water on the top of flood, found everything
almost as smooth as a mill-pond, and got through
in perfect safety. Shortly afterwards we passed
Ledaig Point, the channel between Dunstaffnage
and the big island, and were snugly moored in
Oban Bay by eleven o'clock.

It may be mentioned for the information of
those who would wish to visit the magnificent
scenery of Upper Loch Etive, but who have not
the opportunity of doing so in a yacht, that
this may be done either from Bunawe or Oban ;
the former is ten miles nearer to the head of
the loch, and a boat may be hired for the day's
excursion for about the same number of shillings.
A very early start will be advisable, as there is
fully twenty miles sailing or rowing, and if in
addition to this the tourist is desirous of walking some distance up Glen Etive, he will find
the hours of the longest summer's day well-nigh

exhausted before he gets back to Bunawe. If,
on the other hand, he prefers starting from Oban,
he will have the advantage of a better boat and
more experienced pilot than could be procured
at Bunawe, but he will also have ten miles
farther to go, and will require to remain all
night at the head of Loch Etive in a cottar's
or gamekeeper's house, unless he has had the
precaution to take a portable tent along with
him. This latter plan, however, although more
expensive and occupying longer time, undoubtedly
affords the best opportunities of studying and
enjoying that unrivalled combination of lake and
mountain scenery; and we feel well assured that
all those who may be induced to repair to the
spot and there fill up for themselves the faint
outline which we have endeavoured to sketch,
will find themselves most amply rewarded for
the time and trouble which the journey may
cost. There are now regular steamers to the head
of Loch Etive, which start from a sheltered bay a
little above Connel Ferry.

We would beg to direct the special attention
of landscape-painters to this most magnificent of
the Scottish sea-lochs; the discomforts attendant
upon a visit to its upper extremity, the fatigue,

rude fare, and hard lodging, would be fully repaid by the images of wild and stern grandeur
with which it would store their portfolios and
enrich their minds ; and we should rejoice to see
its varied and almost unknown beauties presented
to the public by the magic pencils of some of our
great landscape-painters.

BEN CRUACHAN FROM SOUND OF MULL.

BLAVEN FROM THE SOUND OF SLEAT.

CHAPTER IV

CRUISE TO LOCH HOURN

THE majority of tourists are like sheep, always
following a leader and adhering closely to the
beaten track; and so it happens that some of
the finest scenery, even in our own island, is
still almost untrodden and unknown — without
roads, inns, guides, coaches, or steamboats. Yet
a little time and toil is well spent in visiting
such spots; and indifferent living and rough
lodging are amply repaid by the freshness and
magnificence of an almost virgin nature. There
is more scenery of this description on the western

coasts of the counties of Inverness, Ross, and Sutherland than in any other part of Great Britain. There, the shores are indented by a succession of sea-lochs running far up into the land; some wide and spacious, others narrow and winding; some with undulating banks green with rich pasture, or thickly clothed with natural wood; some laving the feet of steep mountains, with bold gray crags breaking through the purple bloom of the heather, or the golden glow of the deer-grass and bracken. Between Cape Wrath and the Sound of Mull there are more than twenty such lochs, many of which are never visited by steamers, with but footpaths or rough bridle-tracks along their shores, and with no token of human habitation, except, at long intervals, the house of a sheep farmer, a shepherd's shieling, the hut of a charcoal-burner, or a gamekeeper's cottage. Yet the scenery around some of these arms of the western sea is unequalled elsewhere in Great Britain, and not surpassed even in Switzerland or the Tyrol. At different periods during the last ten years, we have visited most of them; and we now propose to offer some description of Loch Hourn—one of the most beautiful and inaccessible—which we were induced to visit in autumn, by hearing an animated description of the grandeur of its scenery from a Highland gentleman resident in the neighbourhood, whose debtor we have ever since considered ourselves.

If our readers will refer to a good map of Scotland, they will observe a long narrow channel called the Sound of Sleat, separating the island of Skye from the mainland of Inverness-shire; and, about half-way up, and on the east side of the Sound, a deep indentation in the mainland, wide at the entrance but contracting at its upper extremity, and confined on each side by a barrier of lofty mountains:—this is Loch Hourn, or the Loch of Hell, easily distinguished from Loch Nevis (the Loch of Heaven), a few miles to the south of it, by the noble outlines of the lofty Ben Sgriol, which sweeps down in grand curves to the water's edge, and seems to guard the entrance of the loch.

We started on our voyage to Loch Hourn from the little town of Tobermory, in the island of Mull, in a small cutter yacht, built by Fyfe, of Fairlie, and the winner of several cups at the Clyde regattas; having previously taken on board as pilot an ancient Celt, yclept Hector McKinnon,

who had been for forty years a sailor, and who
undertook to bring us in safety to the anchorage
of Barrisdale, half-way up the loch. A strong
adverse tide detained us for a long time in passing
the lofty promontory of Ardnamurchan, which
marks the northern entrance of the Sound of
Mull. At the foot of this promontory lies a
small rocky island, of which our pilot related
the following legend, which, so far as we know,
has not yet found its way into any guide-book :—
" In days of yore, the owner of this islet was a
handsome young fellow, with no fortune but his
good looks and this fragment of sea-beaten rock.
However, he contrived to win the heart of a fair
lady in a distant part of the country, but her
relations were opposed to the match until they
had ascertained what settlement the lover was
able to make. Accordingly, they asked him what
dowry he would give his bride ; to which he
replied that, in his own country, he possessed
an island which seven ploughs could not till,
although they ploughed for a whole year, and
that this he was willing to bestow on his bride.
Nothing could be more satisfactory, and the
young pair were happily married. On reaching
her husband's country, the lady was naturally

anxious to see the fertile island which he had so generously bestowed upon her. On which he showed her the barren crag at the foot of Ardnamurchan Point, and asked whether she thought that seven ploughs could cultivate it although they ploughed for a whole year."

After passing Ardnamurchan, the wind fell to a very moderate breeze, and we had a pleasant, though somewhat tedious sail, passing close to the islands of Muck and Eigg, and in sight of the purple mountains of Rum, and the steep summits of the Coolin hills in Skye. We had made an early start from Tobermory, but it was evening before we came to anchor opposite the farmhouse of Barrisdale, which occupies a picturesque situation among a group of old trees at the foot of a mountain that slopes steeply upwards above a bay at the head of outer Loch Hourn. The outer loch is a spacious sheet of water about twelve miles in length, overshadowed by dark mountain masses; but, fine as it is, it serves only as the vestibule to the exquisite scenery of Little, or Upper, Loch Hourn, which branches off from it in an easterly direction. On the morning succeeding our arrival, we rowed ashore and called on Mr. McDonell, whose ancestors, for several

generations, have occupied the farm of Barrisdale.
He himself is a hale, handsome old gentleman,
descended from those Macdonells of Glengarry
whose domains once extended from Loch Hourn
to Fort Augustus, but are now divided between
Mr. Ellice and Mr. Baird, a rich ironmaster,
who possesses the whole country around Loch
Hourn and between it and Loch Nevis.

From our anchorage the loch seemed entirely
landlocked, and divided into three bays, surrounded by mountains. To the seaward stretched
a wide expanse of water, overshadowed on one
side by the lofty Ben Sgriol, whose lower slopes
are thickly clothed with natural wood, which
adorns, without enervating, the grand curves of
the mountain ; and on the other by green hills,
broken by gray crags, and furrowed by ravines,
beyond which tower sharp rocky pinnacles rising
from wild corries, the haunts of the red-deer
and the eagle. Such a green hill-side with a deep
corrie behind it, over which frowns a steep serrated
ridge, rose immediately above our anchorage.
Ladhar bheinn, the highest point of this ridge,
is 3343 feet above the sea, or nearly as high
as Snowdon. To the south-east, we looked
into the deep bay of Barrisdale, at the head

of which—rare sight in these wild Highlands
—the mountains separate, and leave room for
a considerable tract of level meadow-land, where
rows of tall poplars, clumps of ancient ash
and plane trees and thriving crops of corn
and turnips, gave a sylvan and almost low-
land aspect to the landscape, offering a striking
contrast to the rugged grandeur of the surrounding scenery. Beyond this strip of meadow-land
rises a noble mountain, varied and picturesque in
outline, with its lower slopes and ravines richly
wooded. The whole aspect and character of the
scenery around Barrisdale is more Tyrolese than
Scotch.

Our venerable pilot proved exceedingly com-
municative of his nautical experiences, especially
under the exhilarating influence of a glass of
whisky, and this morning he spun us the following extraordinary, and not very credible, yarn :—

"Many years ago, he was at Riga with his ship,
and he, along with several of his comrades, went
ashore, where—sailor-like—they got very drunk.
Hector was the worst of the lot; and as his
shipmates could not induce him to follow them,
they allowed him to shift for himself, and returned
to their ship. Left to himself, he staggered along

for some distance, and at length fell insensible
in the street. At this time cholera was raging
in Riga; and just as Hector fell, the dead cart
was making its daily rounds, when, seeing him
lying speechless and motionless in the street, its
conductor at once concluded that he had fallen
a victim to the plague, threw a rope round his
body, and tossed him into the cart. He was
restored to consciousness by being pitched out of
the dead cart into a large pit nearly filled with
bodies in various stages of decomposition, and with
difficulty managed to writhe himself clear of the
lime which was thrown over them in considerable
quantities. Fully recalled to his senses, but
almost paralysed by the horrors of his position,
he at last, after many efforts, contrived to struggle
out of the pit, and make his way back to the town;
where his appearance—pale, ghastly, and sprinkled
over with the lime which he had not been able
wholly to avoid—struck terror into every one,
so that he had clear streets as—literally risen from
the dead—he tottered along, and with difficulty
regained his ship, where it was some time before
he recovered from the effects of the drunken frolic
so nearly brought to a horrible termination."

We think that this anecdote of Hector's might

be admirably worked by temperance lecturers, to
whom we beg most respectfully to present it.

But—to return from Riga to Loch Hourn—
beautiful as Barrisdale is, we had yet by far the
finest part of the loch to explore; so, getting into
our punt, we started, a little past eleven o'clock,
to row to the head of it, a distance of more than
six miles from our anchorage.   Several small rocky
islands lie across the entrance of the upper loch,
above which it forms three reaches, connected by
narrows, through which the tide runs with great
violence.   Little, or Upper Loch Hourn, runs nearly
east and west, forming an obtuse angle with the outer
and larger loch.   Its northern shores are bounded
by picturesque mountains, nearly 3000 feet high,
covered for two-thirds of their height with the
most lavish growth of natural wood—birch, ash,
oak, and alder.   The mountains on the opposite
shore are about the same height, but more rugged
and bare, though covered in many places with good
pasturage, and dotted over with trees, singly or in
groups.   At various spots on both banks there
are crags projecting boldly into the water, and,
in some instances, rising precipitously for a couple
of hundred feet.   Some of these are masses of
bare rock; some have tufts of heather, or bunches

of fern, growing from their crevices; others are almost buried beneath luxuriant foliage; and one —a most picturesque crag—bears a solitary old Scotch fir-tree on its topmost pinnacle. There is no monotony—the great fault of the scenery of most of our Scottish lochs—about Loch Hourn, but, on the contrary, an endless, inexhaustible variety and grandeur. There is the sublimity of the upper reach of Loch Etive, in Argyleshire, where its narrow waters are darkened by the huge bulk of Ben Cruachan and Ben Starav, combined with the quieter beauty of the Trossachs, Windermere, or the Lower Lake of Killarney. At several points there are waterfalls, tumbling over a face of bare rock, or sparkling through a thick fringe of foliage, and here and there, along the shore, the thatched cottage of a fisherman, with brown nets hung up to dry. After a long pull, we reached Loch Hourn-head, where we left our boat, and walked for a couple of miles up the beautiful pass that leads to Tomdown Inn, and to the town of Inverness, the former sixteen, and the latter sixty-seven miles from Loch Hourn-head. A bare precipitous mountain, called Buidhe Bheinn, towers above the head of the loch, and on its flanks, to the left of the road leading up the pass, is a

deep ravine, into which falls a lofty and picturesque cascade ; while. about a mile farther up, is a
quiet little lake with a broad green margin of
rushes, through which flows the stream that runs
into Loch Hourn-head. From what we saw of this
pass, we feel convinced that it would well repay
the adventurous pedestrian. On our way back to
the cutter, we were much detained by the strength
of the flood tide, had to hug the shore to avoid its
force, and had several desperate spurts against it
in the Narrows, where it ran like a mill-race. We
had kept along the south shore in ascending, and
now, in returning, we kept close to the northern or
wooded bank, and had again occasion to admire
the profusion and bounty of nature, in clothing
these steep mountain-slopes with such a close and
graceful mantle of varied shades of green. It was
past six o'clock when we reached our vessel, not at
all sorry to rest, after a six hours' pull against a
strong tide. The waters of Upper Loch Hourn
seem absolutely alive with fish. With a single
line of small cord, lightly leaded, and a couple of
salmon flies, we caught, during the short time we
could spare for fishing, seven dozen of fish—lythe,
sethe, and small cod—varying in weight from half
a pound to two pounds and a half. On the rocks

along the shore there is an inexhaustible supply of bait in the shape of mussels, so that to those fond of sea-fishing Loch Hourn offers great attractions, in addition to the charms of its unrivalled scenery.

We now request our readers to accompany us from Loch Hourn through the Sound of Sleat to Portree in Skye, and afterwards to Stornoway in the Lewis.

We left our anchorage at Barrisdale at the entrance of outer Loch Hourn, early on a fine autumn morning. There was but little wind, and that blowing right up the loch, so that we had a dead beat till we got into the Sound of Sleat, in the course of which we got occasional glimpses of the glorious scenery of the upper loch, and more thorough views of the fine mountains and corries that border the shores of the outer and wider arm. There is a rock nearly in the middle of the entrance to the loch, but always above water, to the westward of which the water is shallow for about a cable's length. It will be avoided by bringing Ardnaslish Point on, or nearly on, the Point of Sleat. Once in the Sound of Sleat, the wind was fair, and freshened as the day advanced, so that we bowled along at a rapid rate with all sail set and everything drawing; passing on the

mainland side the beautiful Bay of Glenelg with
its ruined barrack, built to overawe the Highlands,
the entrance to the picturesque but squally Loch
Duich, and the fine scenery around Loch Alsh;
and on the other side, the lofty mountains of Skye,
towering above the narrow waters of the Strait.
Near Kyleakin the wind became light and baffling,
and for a time we were becalmed; but a brisk
though adverse breeze springing up, we had a fine
beat through the Narrows where the tide runs
six miles an hour.   But wind and weather are
proverbially fickle in these narrow and landlocked
waters, and you may have sun and shower, clear sky
and dense mist, a calm, a breeze, and a gale of wind,
all within the space of twenty-four hours.   Scarcely
had we got through the Narrows, when the breeze
again fell, though as night darkened down it rose
a little.   But it was five o'clock on Friday morning before we reached Portree, though we had left
Loch Hourn at ten on Thursday forenoon, and had
carried a fine breeze with us from the mouth of the
loch to Balmacara.   In the course of the day we
passed two ruined castles, one on the mainland,
and the other in Skye, both most attractive in
ruins, and offering admirable subjects to the
sketcher.   The one, Eilan Donan Castle, stands

near the entrance of Loch Duich. It is by far the
larger and more ancient building of the two, and
was the chief stronghold of the Mackenzies of
Kintail, built in the time of Alexander the Second,
as a defence against the ravages of the Northmen.
The other ruin, Castle Moil, is situated close to
Kyleakin, and is most picturesquely perched on a
beetling and sea-beat crag. If the wind happens
to be off the Skye land when the yachtsman is
passing this old fortalice, he may perchance have
cause to remember it, for sudden squalls rush down
like eagles from that wild highland, and while
bowling along with a steady breeze he may
suddenly catch a puff that will compel him to luff
up sharp, and perhaps lower his peak and haul up
his main-tack. With the wind either blowing
from the Skye land, or out of Loch Duich, the
steersman had better keep his weather eye open.

Portree—the King's Harbour—so called from
James the Fifth having landed there when on a
visit to the western islands, is well sheltered, and has
good holding ground, the depth varying from five to
fourteen fathoms. The entrance lies between two
lofty headlands, and there is no danger, except a
rock partly above water, about half a cable's
length from the point on your starboard hand on

entering. The most interesting object in the neighbourhood of Portree,—which is in general very bleak and sombre,—is the Storr hill about seven miles distant in a northerly direction, which will be found fully described in the first cruise.

We remained only a single day in Portree, and at five o'clock on a stormy September morning, after the usual preliminary plunge over the side, started for Stornoway, the capital of the Lewis. Our course was about north and by east, and as the wind was blowing nearly from that direction we had the prospect of a long and stormy beat before us. With this wind, there is generally a heavy sea in the Minch, as the broad channel between Lewis and the mainland is called, especially when the tides which run pretty strong here happen to meet it. The distance from Portree to Stornoway is upwards of fifty miles, and the sail is a very interesting one, commanding fine and varied views of the bold cliffs and hills of Skye; the barren rocks of Raasay; the lochs and mountains of the mainland; the islands of Lewis and Harris; and the distant and mountainous group of North Uist, Benbecula, and South Uist, the last conspicuous by the bold conical peak of Heela, which rises nearly 2000 feet above the sea.

After getting clear of Portree, we had a tedious
beat through the Sound of Raasay, and had ample
opportunities to study and admire the bold line of
cliffs that stretches from Portree-heads all the way
to the Point of Aird, the northernmost promontory
of Skye. The Storr with its strange fantastic
pinnacles and coronet of precipices, looked like
some ruined castle of Titans; and farther to the
north we got a glimpse of the rocks that encircle
Quiraing, the greatest geological curiosity in Skye.

On leaving the Sound of Raasay, we made a
long tack towards the Scottish coast in the direction of the peninsula between Gairloch and Loch
Ewe, which seemed in the distance a long low
line of land covered with the most beautiful
pearly haze. The lofty mountains around Loch
Maree, and in the district of Gairloch, were seen
to great advantage, and looked more and more
imposing as we drew gradually nearer to them.
On the opposite tack we had to contend against
both wind and tide, and took a long time to
weather the Skye land. Off the Island of Trotta,
to the north of the Point of Aird, so strong was
the tide, that for some time we did little more
than hold our own. Soon afterwards the wind
began to freshen considerably, and towards even-

ing it blew half a gale; but we hove the little
cutter to, double-reefed the mainsail, reefed the
foresail, reefed the bowsprit, and shifted jibs,
after which she behaved beautifully, going over
the seas like a duck and shipping no heavy water.
Not far from the mouth of Loch Seaforth in Lewis
— a splendid harbour capable of containing the
whole British Navy - - lies a curious group of
basaltic rocks called the Shiant Islands, rejoicing
in the unpronounceable names of Garivelan, Ilan
Wirrey, and Ilanakilly. To the westward of the
first-named islet there are three or four rocks
above water, the highest of which is called Galti-
more; and to it a good berth must be given
when passing to the westward, as a quarter of a
mile west of it lies a rock which dries at half-ebb.

By the time we had passed the Shiant Islands,
night had fallen and the weather was exceedingly
bad, blowing a gale and raining heavily. We
had two of the best harbours in the Hebrides
under our lee — Loch Seaforth and East Loch
Tarbert—and for a moment we thought of running
into one of these for shelter, but soon—determined
not to be beat—we made up our minds to hold
on and thrash the little beauty through it. We
had the guidance of the bright fixed light on

the island of Scalpa, and when we lost that we
sighted the Stornoway light; and at length, after
twenty-three hours of a hard struggle against
wind and sea, we had the satisfaction of dropping
our anchor at six o'clock on Sunday morning
in the sheltered waters of Stornoway Bay, wet
through and thoroughly tired, but highly pleased
at having made out our destination in spite of
wind and weather.

Stornoway is a spacious and excellent harbour;
and in beating in you have only to remember to
give Arnish Point and also the Point of Holm a
good berth. The best anchorage is above the
little island near the town at the head of the
bay. All hands being thoroughly tired, it was
mid-day before we turned out of our berths. On
getting on deck, the most prominent object that
met our eyes was the Elizabethan mansion of
the late Sir James Matheson, then proprietor of
the Lewis, built on a green slope, and surrounded
by slowly-rising but healthy-looking plantations.
It stands close to the thriving town of Stornoway,
from which it is separated only by a narrow
creek almost dry at low water. The west side
of the bay is occupied by the grounds belonging
to Stornoway Castle. Nature has supplied a

K

succession of rocky knolls of different heights, clothed with heather, grass, and ferns, and indented by a number of creeks and gravelly bays; while Art—at an expense of £15,000 or £20,000—has clothed these knolls with a great variety of wood—pine, ash, elder, birch, elm, holly, etc.—and cut a profusion of winding walks, laid out with great taste, and kept in perfect order. Some of the creeks are highly picturesque, especially that formed by the estuary of the little river Creed, across the mouth of which lies a small rocky islet covered, like the rest of the shore, with heather, grass, and ferns. The wood which Sir James has planted on the pleasure-grounds attached to his castle has been reared in despite of nature, and, as before mentioned, at immense expense. It was of about thirteen years' growth when we saw it, and yet none of the pines were above twelve feet high. But, though stunted in growth, most of the trees seemed healthy and thriving.

No stranger should visit Stornoway without ascending the highest of the knolls in the castle grounds, which rises just above the best anchorage in the bay. Perhaps with the exception of Killiney Hill near Kingston, and the Calton Hill

in Edinburgh, no spot in the United Kingdom
of equally easy ascent commands so extensive
and varied a prospect; while the extreme clear-
ness of the autumnal atmosphere in this northern

SGURR NAN GILLEAN FROM PORTREE.

locality lends remarkable distinctness even to the
most distant objects. The afternoon on which
we climbed this hill was calm and clear, so that
we saw the view to the best advantage.

Close at hand, we commanded the fine bay
of Stornoway; the residence and grounds of Sir
James Matheson; the wild, brown, undulating,

moorland region to the westward of the bay; the
well-cultivated peninsula on which the town of
Stornoway stands; Loch Tua or Broad Bay, on
whose sandy shore a heavy surf was breaking:
and the flat bleak moor stretching away to the
northward of it. To the south lay the mountains of Harris; and beyond, to the eastward
and southward, a wide expanse of sea, bounded by
that unrivalled range of mountains that stretches
almost from Cape Wrath to the entrance of Loch
Ewe. In the extreme distance, Cape Wrath itself
was visible, low and blue, on the very verge of
the horizon.

The second day after our arrival in Stornoway,
I parted with much regret from my good friend
A, with whom I had enjoyed a delightful three
weeks' cruise among the islands and lochs of the
west coast of Scotland, I going south in the
good steamer *Clansman*, and he beginning his
preparations for taking his little cutter round
Cape Wrath and to the Orkney Islands, by procuring a pilot, getting his cockpit boarded over,
and otherwise having everything made as snug
as possible.

An amusing incident preceded our parting:
A was anxious to provide himself with a warm

pea-jacket, as the nights were getting cold, and
I accompanied him in his search through various
shops in Stornoway. But in none of them could
he find a jacket large enough to cover his goodly
proportions; so that he had to order one to be
made, and the amazement of the tailor who
measured him—a little shrivelled specimen of
humanity—was ludicrous, when he looked at his
measuring tape and read forty-three inches round
the chest, and thirty-two round the waist—the
Celts in these parts never running so large.
However, he was loud in his admiration of A's
athletic proportions.

EGILSEY CHURCH, ORKNEY.

WITCH MOUNTAIN, BÖMMEL FIORD.

CHAPTER V

A YACHT CRUISE FROM LERWICK TO BERGEN

IN former days the coasts of Britain were often ravaged by the adventurous arms of the Scandinavian Vikings, whose war-galleys were for three centuries the scourge and the terror of Europe. Olaf of Norway, in one of his plundering expeditions, destroyed London Bridge, and little more than six centuries have elapsed since the Orkney and Shetland Isles, the counties of Caithness and Sutherland, the Hebrides, and the western coast of Scotland from Cape Wrath to the Mull of Cantire, were subject to the sway of the Norwegian crown. Traces of that rule yet remain in the common speech of the Shetlanders, among whom nearly two hundred words of Norwegian origin are still in ordinary use. No one, therefore, acquainted with the history of the past, can fail to look upon Norway with a lively interest from the stirring historical associations which yet linger around her; and, when to these are added the beauty, variety, and grandeur of her mountains and fiords, it must be admitted that a voyage to the home of the ancient sea-kings, and the cradle of that stalwart Norman race which gave a king and a nobility to England, presents attractions of no ordinary kind. Such a voyage too is easily accomplished during the summer season, even in a vessel of very moderate dimensions, though we should not exactly like to attempt it in an eight-tonner like the lively little *Pet*, which twice bore her clever and adventurous owner from England to the Baltic. Only a narrow sea separates the Shetland Islands from the opposite coasts of Europe, and no better point of departure can be selected for a yacht-cruise to Norway than the safe and spacious harbour of Lerwick, from which, on a bright July morning, we set sail, bound for the mouth of the Bömmel Fiord. Our vessel was a stout cutter of thirty-five tons, a capital sea-boat, manned by four hands and a steward, and carrying besides, her

owner and three friends, amply provided with
fishing-rods, rifles, sketching materials, and other
requisites for making the most of a short visit
to "Gamle Norge."

It was eight o'clock when we took our
departure, and, although we had a fresh and
favourable breeze, many hours elapsed before
we lost sight of the magnificent promontory
of Noss Head, which rises abruptly 700 feet
above the waves of the northern ocean. At nine
next morning we were in sight of the rocky
island of Udsire, conspicuous from its twin red-
painted light-towers. On getting close to the
island, we hove to, and hoisted the signal for a
pilot, and soon observed a small fragile skiff
sailing out from the island to board us. There
was a heavy sea running, and, in the trough
of the waves, we could see nothing but the top
of her mast. The pilot was a remarkably good-
looking young fellow, with fair hair, bright complexion, and tall athletic figure. After taking
him on board, we stood away for the Bömmel
Fiord, the entrance to which is guarded on either
side by low barren rocks, one hundred acres of
which would scarcely feed a single sheep. With
the exception of this utter sterility, the general

aspect of the scenery at this point much resembles
that of a sea-loch in the Western Highlands of
Scotland. As we advanced, however, the landscape improved ; clean wooden cottages with tiled
roofs were perched among the rocks, and grass
and trees began to appear. We passed several
gaudily-painted vessels descending the fiord. One
of them, in a coat of green, black, and yellow,
all of the brightest tints, and carrying every
sail set, was yet a most picturesque-looking craft.
and would have delighted a painter's eye.

Near the snug little village and harbour of
Mösterhaven (above which the fiord assumes the
name of Hardanger), we observed a most primitive-
looking lighthouse built of wood, painted white,
and with a tiled roof, perched upon a cliff but
little elevated above the level of the fiord. Close
to Mösterhaven our pilot landed, and we procured
another who was to convey us first to Bondhus
on the Moranger Fiord, and afterwards to Vik,
at the head of the Hardanger. The pilot who
brought us from Udsire to Mösterhaven, a distance
of twenty-seven miles, had inherited a double
portion of the plundering propensities of his
piratical ancestors. He had the assurance to
demand £2 for his four hours' work, and we

ultimately succeeded in beating him down to 7½
dollars, an exorbitant sum for all that he had
done. Like most of the Norwegian pilots, he
asked for "schnapps" the moment he came on
board, and tossed off a glass of strong Scotch
whisky as if it had been water. His successor
was an old man, still hale and active, apparently
about sixty years of age, but, according to his
own account, seventy-five, with a face whose skin,
in colour and texture, resembled old parchment
from constant exposure to the weather. He wore
a sou'-wester hat, an old patched jacket, trousers
of coarse gray stuff, and a waistcoat of pilot cloth,
over which the trousers were buttoned, and he
brought with him a bag made of coarse sacking
which contained his pea-jacket and other articles
of clothing.

Above Mösterhaven the landscape becomes
finer and more varied : the broad bosom of the
fiord is dotted over with islands ; innumerable
bays and creeks indent its shores ; small hamlets
and villages nestle in all the more sheltered and
fertile spots ; the hills and crags are fringed
with wood, and high mountain peaks and snow-
crowned ridges begin to appear in the background.
The distance from Mösterhaven to the village of

Bondhus at the head of the Moranger Fiord is
about fifty miles, and at the point where that
fiord diverges from the Hardanger, the scenery
is particularly grand and impressive. A green
wooded promontory stretches almost across the
opening of the Moranger, so that entrance seems
at first sight impossible. On this promontory
stands the small village of Ænaes, while beyond,
steep mountains shoot boldly up from the fiord
with scarped and furrowed sides, but with trees
springing from every ledge where a little soil
supplies nourishment for their roots. On the
same side, and a little above Ænaes, is a very
lofty and precipitous rock-face dipping sheer down
into the fiord; and about a mile farther up a
most magnificent waterfall, clothing a vast crag
with a flowing drapery of snowy foam. We
estimated its height at about 300 feet, and its
breadth at the widest part at 200. It rushes
over the cliff from amidst a fringe of foliage in
three separate streams perpendicularly for the
first 150 feet, and then dashes into the fiord
over a long steep slope of jagged rocks. The
lower fall spreads out to a great breadth, and
brightens the dark cliff with wreaths and whirls
of sparkling foam, which find rest at length after

their vexed career in the green waters of the
Moranger. The vast water-power here developed
has been turned to some account by the Norwegians. The lower fall is divided into two
portions by a green promontory which juts out
into the fiord, and on this stands a rude and
primitive sawmill with stone foundations, but
built of wood and roofed with shingles. Near
it is a still ruder and smaller mill—something
like those still in use in Shetland—moved by a
small horizontal wheel placed under the shed in
which the mill-stones work. Passing Ænaes and
its magnificent waterfall, we continued our course
up the Moranger, and soon opened on our right
the village of Bondhus with its narrow valley
closed in by steep mountains, between two of
which lies the glacier of Bondhus, rifted and
seamed by chasms and crevices, and with the
blue gleam of its ice catching the eye, and marking it out from the adjoining snowfield of the
Folgefonde. Our pilot, unfortunately, turned out
a thorough impostor. He had never been up
the Moranger Fiord, and, instead of anchoring
at Bondhus, took us up to Fladbö at the head
of the other branch of the Moranger, and then
gave orders to let go the anchor close to the

shore, on which a pretty stiff breeze was blowing at the time. The result was that we got no bottom with forty fathoms of chain out, and were

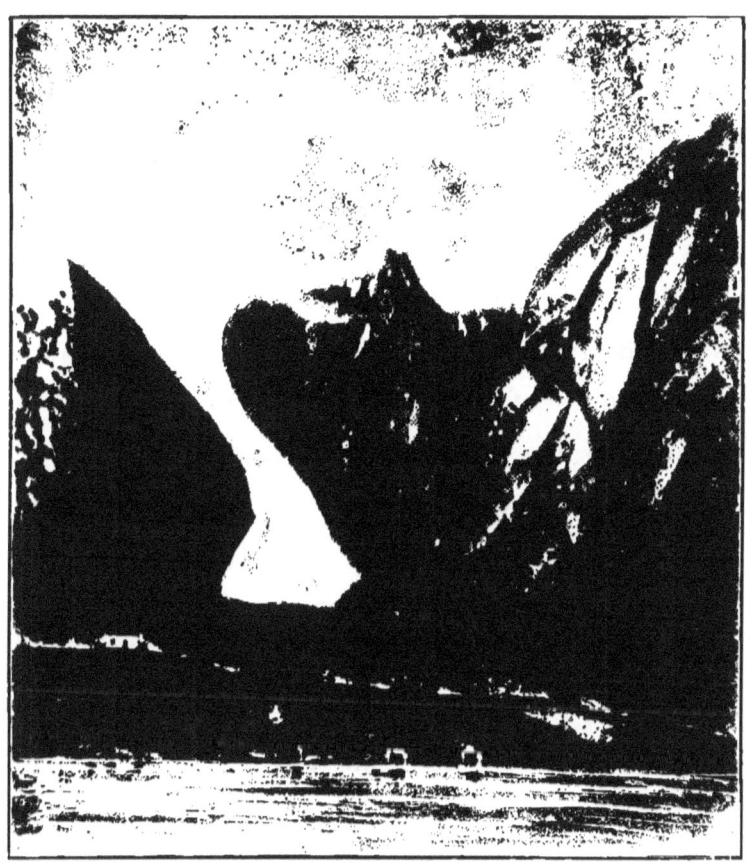

BONDHUS GLACIER.

nearly driven on shore owing to his ignorance and presumption. A Norwegian obligingly rowed out from Fladbö, and told us there was no anchorage, and that we had already passed Bondhus,

a fact which seemed greatly to astonish our
pilot. but, after the specimen we had had of his
knowledge of the Moranger, it was impossible
to trust him to bring us to at Bondhus, so we
determined to retrace our course to the Hardanger,
with which he seemed somewhat better acquainted.
It was a beautiful calm evening when we re-
entered the Hardanger, and the view looking
back towards the mountains around Æmaes was
very striking. One dark conical mass in particular
stood boldly forward, with its sharp peak streaked
with patches of snow, while behind rose a noble
mountain range sweeping round in a grand curve,
its summits clothed with heavy masses of snow.
Here we were becalmed for nearly twelve hours,
and then, getting a favourable breeze, rapidly
passed the pretty villages of Jondal and Strande-
barm, and, at Vikor, entered a long reach of the
Hardanger, which had all the appearance of a
large inland sea. There is a good deal of sameness
in this part of the scenery, but still it is very
picturesque and pleasing. Green swells of land,
generally well wooded, rising from sweet pastoral
valleys; and, beyond these, steep crags and lofty
summits with specks of snow brightening the
dulness of their gray peaks.

A little above Vikor, on the same side of the fiord, is a splendid waterfall, several hundred feet in height, and with a great body of water. It is almost buried in foliage, and its white foaming stream contrasts finely with the green clothing of the mountain-side. We heard the roar of this cataract long before we came abreast of it. It is the third grand waterfall pouring into the Hardanger; as, besides that near Ænaes, there is another above Youdal, not far from the spot where a magnificent range of precipices of dark purple rock overhang the deep waters of the fiord. Waterfalls, indeed, form a principal feature in the landscape of the Hardanger; for, in addition to the three principal falls, innumerable minor cascades —from the tiny thread of foam lost in mist before it reaches the bottom of the rock up to the size of the Fall of Foyers—lend their tribute to its waters. Many of the houses along the banks of the fiord are fantastically painted, generally in the brightest colours. We observed one, the front of which was painted white, the roof red, and the gable end red with a white line around it; another had the upper story red and the under white; and many were entirely red. There is not much level ground; but every available space is taken advantage of for building or farming. The want of animal life on the Hardanger is very striking. We saw but few birds, and these were so shy that they would scarcely let us get within rifle-shot.

Near the pretty village of Utne, one of the sweetest spots on the Hardanger, the fiord takes a sharp and sudden bend to the south, and the scenery increases in boldness and beauty. Utne, with its clean, brightly-painted wooden houses, occupies a beautiful situation at the mouth of a green wooded valley on the south-eastern shore of the fiord. Opposite to it is the opening of the Eide Fiord, and above it that of the Sör Fiord, two branches of the great Hardanger, the last of which stretches away to the glaciers and snowfields of the Folgefonde, one of the mightiest accumulations of ice and snow in Norway. We were much amused this morning by our aged Palinurus. After a capital breakfast on beef, biscuits, and coffee, he asked for tobacco; and, on being offered some Latakia, seized a handful that would have filled half a dozen pipes, and deliberately crammed it into his mouth. Certainly for a man of seventy-five he had a wonderful digestion.

Beyond the opening of the Sör Fiord the Hardanger again stretches in a north-eastern

direction, which it maintains as far as Vik. The
view up the Sör Fiord is superb; a narrow reach
of water trending away for miles between snow-
capped mountains, those on the southern side
being crowned with the eternal snows of the
Folgefonde. Passing the entrance of the Sör Fiord,
we stretched away for our destination, the village
of Vik, still ten or twelve miles distant. On
either side of us were lofty mountains, those on
the southern shore precipitous and barren, and
those on the opposite bank sloping up in a succession of rocky terraces thickly clothed with
wood. The weather on the Hardanger is very
variable: calms and breezes from every point of
the compass succeeding each other with startling
suddenness. Towards its termination the fiord
divides into three branches; the most northerly
leading to Ulvik, the middle to Öse, and the
most southern and principal to Vik, one of the
post stations on the road from Bergen to Christiania. That part of the Hardanger Fiord which
extends from Odde at the head of the Sör Fiord
to Vik is in shape almost a crescent about thirty
miles in length. From Odde by land across the
snowfields of the Folgefonde to Bondhus at the
head of the Moranger Fiord is only twelve miles,

and yet the distance by water cannot be less than sixty miles, which may give some idea of the extent to which the Hardanger and its various branches and windings indent and diversify the surface of the country.

Shortly before reaching Vik, we obtained a splendid view up the dark and narrow gorge of the Seimadal, the distance being filled up by the snowy coronal of the Hallens Jökelen, upwards of 5000 feet high.

We cast anchor at Vik on the 19th of July, just forty-eight hours after we had entered the Bömmel Fiord. We were anchored about a cable's length from the shore in twenty-five fathoms. The great difficulty in the Hardanger is to find anchorage, owing to the extreme depth of the water, varying from 100 to 200 fathoms, even quite near the shore. The inn at Vik stands close to the water's edge, and (for Norway) is clean and comfortable, though those travellers who expect carpeted rooms, cushioned chairs and sofas, and the other luxuries of civilised hotels, would probably consider its accommodation very contemptible. A little farther inland are the village of Eidfiord, and a quaint old church said to have been built long ago by a Norwegian

lady as an expiation for having murdered her husband. The approach to the village leads across a narrow plain studded with stunted birch trees, then there is a short ascent and another level dotted over with the same scanty vegetation. These flats, about a mile and a half wide, are hemmed in on each side by lofty and precipitous mountains, whose summits, however, are rather lumpy and rounded in outline. Across the valley stretches transversely an enormous mound, three or four hundred feet high, which appears to have once formed the terminal moraine of a glacier. It is now clothed with birch and fir trees, and cut through by the deep and rapid torrent which rushes from the lake of Sæbo into the Hardanger Fiord.

In the evening five young Cantabs arrived at the inn, having just returned from an excursion to the Vöring Foss, the finest waterfall in Europe. They told us that they had travelled overland from Christiania, boating and walking most of the way. They complained bitterly of the difficulty of getting sufficient food, and assured us that but for their fishing-rods they must have been nearly starved. We invited them on board, and set before them a cold round of beef and

sundry bottles of Bass's ale. and certainly the way
in which they disposed of both meat and drink
bore ample testimony to the justice of their
complaints. and gave an appalling idea of the
poverty of Norwegian fare.   The round never
recovered that onslaught.   Afterwards, we all enjoyed a sociable smoke on deck, and parted late
in the evening; they to go on early next morning
to Odde, at the head of the Sör Fiord, and thence
across the snows of the Folgefonde to the glacier
of Bondhus, and we to prepare for an equally
early start to the Vöring Foss.

At half-past five next morning we commenced
operations by a plunge into the cold green waters
of the Hardanger from the deck of the cutter,
while two of our acquaintances of the preceding
evening were taking a "header" from the end
of the wooden quay near the hotel, much to the
astonishment and admiration of an assembled
knot of Norwegians.

At half-past six we started for the Vöring
Foss, each of us having a guide and a pony;
and, after a pleasant ride of a mile, reached the
beautiful lake of Sæbo, where we embarked in
one boat, while our guides and ponies got into
another and heavier one.   We were most fortu-

nate in a day; the sky was bright and almost cloudless, and the sun warm without being scorching. The huge mass of the moraine cut through by the impetuous torrent of the Lundaro Elv stretches across the northern extremity of the lake; on either side lofty and very steep mountains dip sheer down into the clear waters, so that all passage except by boat is impracticable. Near the village of Sæbo the hills on the west side of the lake form a smooth wall of rock, where not a single tree can find a resting-place.

Sæbo is situated at the southern extremity of the lake, on a level alluvial plain where good crops of rye and potatoes are grown. This plain presents its longest side to the water, and gradually narrows inland until terminated by the precipices that overhang the gloomy pass of Hjelmodalen, fit antechamber to the perpetual snows of the Hardanger Fjeld : through this gorge the Hjelmode Elv flows down to the lake of Sæbo, into which it falls on one side of the valley, while on the other runs the Lundaro Elv, which forms the Vöring Foss. The view of the plain and village as we approached them from the lake was very striking : everywhere darkened by the long shadows of the mountains,

except where a narrow belt of bright sunshine
gilded the meadows close to the water. A little
beyond Sæbo we passed a second moraine similar
to that at Vik, but on a smaller scale, and several
of the rocks that we passed in the course of the
day are what are termed *roches moutonnées*,
bearing evident traces of glacier action. After
crossing this moraine, we entered a narrow but
grand rocky defile, which extends for several
miles in an easterly direction to the foot of that
steep and lofty ascent which leads up to the
level of the Vöring Foss. Proceeding up this
for some miles, we came to a wooden bridge of
a very picturesque but exceedingly shaky description, which spans the river, here both deep and
rapid. It is not above four feet wide, and there
is not the slightest vestige of a parapet. Here
we dismounted; the ponies were driven across
singly by the guides, and we followed. Two
and a half hours from Vik brought us to the
little village of Veita, built close to the torrent;
and another half-hour to a smaller hamlet, beyond
which the path becomes exceedingly bad, being
covered with large stones and long slippery slopes
of smooth rock, and in some places so steep that
regular steps have been cut, up which our Norsk

ponies scrambled like cats. On either side huge
blocks of stone detached from the adjacent mountains hem in the path. Some of these are of
enormous size, probably 100 feet square.

On emerging from these rocky masses, we
found ourselves on a narrow strip of meadow-
land, at whose upper extremity the river takes
a sudden bend, and seems to be swallowed up
in the jaws of a narrow pass formed by perpendicular walls of rock, shooting up to a great height
from the water's edge, so that farther progress by
its banks becomes impossible. We now began to
wonder how or where we were to proceed; for on
our left were the river and precipices, while, right
in front, an excessively steep mountain-slope called
the Määbuberg, at least 1200 feet high, seemed to
forbid farther advance, at least to mounted travellers.
But there are no limits to the endurance and ac-
tivity of Norwegian ponies; and whoever wishes
to know what they are capable of performing, and
how perfectly sure-footed they become, should go
to Vik and ride from thence to the Vöring Foss on
the back of one. Cats are nothing to them; and I
have no doubt that one of them might be safely
ridden to the top of Ben Nevis, rough, stony, and
steep as the latter part of that ascent certainly is.

We soon found that the road to the Foss lay up the mountain-face in front of us. A rougher path can scarcely be imagined; it is, however, the only very steep ascent between Vik and the Vöring Foss. One of our party dismounted and walked up, beating his mounted companions by twenty minutes. The ascent of the Määbuberg occupies nearly an hour, but the fatigue is amply repaid by the extensive prospect commanded from its summit. On gaining the top we entered upon a level mossy table-land covered with the common and dwarf birch, and with bushes of the crow- and cloud-berry, from which we had a fine view of the gleaming snowfields of the lofty Jökelen. After riding along this plateau for some miles, our guides conducted us to some shepherds' huts, a little beyond the Vöring Foss, and 2150 feet above the level of the Hardanger. Here we saw our ponies stabled, and afterwards entered the principal Saeter, which boasted of two tolerable apartments. In one of these were hung up a collection of pictures such as we give to children, and an absurd pencil-drawing of some distinguished personage all frogs and frock-coat, but with most ridiculously diminutive legs and feet. We asked for some milk, which was brought to

us in a large wooden bowl about eighteen inches
in circumference and half as much in depth. This
was accompanied by three wooden spoons—one
for each of us; and a sheet of *fladbröd*, as the
ordinary bread of the country is termed. *Fladbröd*
resembles in colour and thickness coarse brown
packing paper, and possesses about an equal
amount of nourishment. It is baked of rye meal
in huge circular cakes, which are first folded
across, and then a second time folded, and in
this form it is kept and sold. For the milk and
fladbröd we paid an *ort*, or 10d. in our money.
On leaving the Saeter we found our guides busily
engaged in supping sour milk curds from a great
wooden bowl, round which they were sociably
seated. We left them engaged in this interesting occupation, and proceeded to a little distance
in order to sketch the Saeter. The fine arts soon
proved a formidable antagonist to the curds, and
we were speedily surrounded by all the guides,
and the whole population of the Saeter, who
watched and criticised our drawings with every
appearance of the greatest interest. Our sketching finished, we lost no time in hastening to the
Vöring Foss, which is about a mile below the
Saeters, and is easily distinguishable from a con-

siderable distance by the light column of glittering
foam that is for ever wreathing upwards from the
abyss. The river appeared to us about as large
as the Clyde at Lanark, and, a little above the
great cataract, there is a lofty and beautiful cascade
which anywhere else would be considered magnificent; but here it only serves as a foil to the great
Vöring Foss. The point from which you see the
fall is at least 150 feet above the spot whence
the river precipitates itself into the boiling pool
beneath, while the perpendicular crag opposite,
crested with stunted birch trees, rises as much
above where you stand. From its summit rushes
a slender thread of foam to add its tiny tribute
to the fathomless abyss 1200 feet below, from
which a thin smoke of spray is perpetually floating
up and overhanging the great cataract with a
dewy curtain, while the dripping rocks opposite
the falling waters reflect the dazzling and varied
hues of a beautiful rainbow. By a little scrambling
a spot may be reached from which the Vöring Foss
is visible in all its unrivalled splendour. Where
the waters first rebound from the precipice, they
are whirled out in wreaths of spray, their edges
just tinged with the most delicate and tender
colours, fining away as they extend till they melt

into air, and ceaselessly revolving in circles of snowy foam till lost in the profound gulf 900 feet below. The purity, the matchless beauty, of these wheels as of white fire no words can describe, nor sketch adequately portray. The Vöring Foss is the very poetry and perfection of waterfalls, and, alone, amply repays the fatigue and expense of a voyage to Norway.

In the afternoon we rode back across the table-land to the summit of the Māābuberg, and, in the descent of the steep and rough zigzags, our ponies displayed their sure-footedness even more conspicuously than during the previous ascent. We reached Vik at six o'clock, having been away for upwards of eleven hours. Even with the aid of ponies and boats no one should attempt the excursion to Vöring Foss who is not prepared for at least two hours' hard walking. We found the charges at Vik extravagant, having to pay for our three guides and ponies 32s. Provisions were also dear: for eggs we paid 9d. a dozen, butter 10d. a pound, and *fladbröd* 1½d. a cake, which, reckoning by weight, is considerably more than the price of the best wheaten bread in Great Britain.

Next day the weather was very bad: the mountains around were either entirely veiled in

clouds, or partially obscured by floating wreaths of
gray mist, while the rain poured in torrents.
In the evening, however, there was a startling
change: the rain ceased, but it blew half a gale
of wind right on shore, and, to our consternation,
we found that our anchor was not holding, and
that we were rapidly drifting on the rocky beach.
We turned all hands up, got sail on the yacht, and
were obliged to beat her out into the fiord through
the darkness and in the teeth of the gale. We
had got so close in-shore that we had scarcely
room to stay the vessel, and had anything gone
wrong when the helm was put down, nothing
could have saved us from driving on the beach.
After gaining a good offing, we again came to
anchor off Vik, but considerably farther from the
shore, and with plenty of chain out, and rode
safely till the morning. We found that the cause
of our former mishap had been the chain cable
getting foul of the anchor-stock. "All's well
that ends well," but we certainly made a narrow
escape from leaving our smart little cutter to
serve as a perpetual model for the boat-builders
of Vik.

Early next morning we bade adieu to Vik, and
sailed for Bergen: the wind was, however, un-

favourable, and we had a tedious voyage down the Hardanger. On leaving it, we entered a perfect labyrinth of rocky islands, through which we were to thread our way to Bergen. Most of these are deeply indented by bays and creeks, and, in general, very barren, though, here and there, a few trees and bushes of purple heather break the gray monotony of their surface. The navigation of the

BOGHOLM SOUND.

numerous and winding channels that surround them is intricate and perplexing, and the white-painted wooden lighthouses perched upon com-manding heights are here absolutely indispensable. Near Bogholm Sound we had a magnificent sunset; a cloudless sky of gold and crimson, against which the fine mountains around Bergen seemed of the deepest purple. The graceful peak of the Lyder-horn and the lofty range of the Lövstakken were especially conspicuous.

The voyage from Vik to Bergen occupied two

days, and early on the morning of the third we
came to anchor at the entrance of the merchant
harbour not far from the quay and custom-house,
in the midst of a crowd of shipping, French,
German, English, and Norsk, the most curious
being the "Jagts" from the northern fisheries,
large vessels with a single mast, a huge square-sail,
and crews of a dozen men each. They are low amid-
ships, curve upwards at the bow and stern, and
the prow rises eight or ten feet above the deck.
Bergen is undoubtedly one of the most picturesque
towns in Europe. There is such variety of colour
and outline, such narrow streets, such quaint old
wooden houses with balconies and projecting roofs,
sometimes built upon quays rising sheer from deep
water, sometimes overhanging short narrow canals
which run up from the harbour, and admit of
vessels lying between the houses. Then there are
the tall old tower of Haco and the ancient palace
of the kings of Norway, recalling the days when
Bergen was a capital,—the dark gray castle of
Fredericksburg on the opposite height,—the long
and lofty range of wooden warehouses which once
received rich merchandise from all parts of the
world when Bergen was one of the five chief ports
of the Hanseatic League.—the varied and ever-

changing character of the shipping in the harbour,
—the fine curve and graceful outline of the mountains that half encircle the city, and the bold
sweep of the deep and sheltered waters that bring
the commerce of distant lands to her threshold—
all combining to form a picture equally delightful
from its natural beauty and romantic associations
with the past.

The first point that we visited after landing was
the fortress of Fredericksburg which crowns a
height rising steeply above the custom-house.
From this commanding position we obtained an
excellent idea of the city and neighbourhood.
Bergen is built partly upon a peninsula facing the
north, and partly along the shores of two deep
bays on the east and west of this peninsula. The
bay on the east is the harbour for merchant ships,
and that on the west for vessels requiring repairs;
the principal shipbuilding yards are also on the
west bay. To the south, an undulating well-
wooded country extends to the base of the mountains, upon whose slopes may be seen the bright-
looking villas of the Bergen merchants. The
warehouses of the Hanse merchants and the castle
of Haco extend along the east side of the merchant
harbour. Pictorially speaking, there is too much

of pure unbroken white in the buildings of Bergen ; but their picturesque shapes, steep roofs, and pointed gables in some degree compensate for this defect. The houses are all built of wood, painted, and, externally at least, kept scrupulously clean. The streets are narrow and ill paved, and beside many of the houses stands a water-barrel as a resource against fire, while at intervals of 100 yards are sentry-boxes for the watchmen. The old and rude system of water-barrels seems likely to be soon superseded by fire-plugs ; for in some of the streets we saw notices of the position of those admirable safeguards for a wooden town. The last fire destroyed 180 houses, and the spot where it raged may still be distinguished by freshness of the tiles on the roofs of the houses that have replaced those which were then destroyed. For the future, all houses built in Bergen must be constructed of brick or stone ; and some of those which we saw in process of erection to the south of the merchant harbour were in conformity with this new regulation. Their construction is very curious : the inner shell is of wood, above that is a rude sheathing of birch bark, and over all a facing of brick sometimes coated with Roman cement.

With the exception of cigars, fish, and Norwegian skiffs, everything is exceedingly dear, and Mr. Greig, the English consul, informed us that, within his remembrance, prices had increased threefold. For a coarse Norsk knife with carved wooden handle, fifteen shillings were demanded, and for a small card-case, also in carved wood, such as might have been purchased in Switzerland for a couple of francs, we were charged nine shillings. But, besides being the dearest, Bergen is also the rainiest of Norwegian towns. We have been in a glen in the Island of Skye, yclept Glen Sligachan (a perfect Shibboleth to English lips), in which we were told that the oldest inhabitant could not remember a day without a shower, and truly, judging from our five days' experience, we can believe the same of Bergen. An umbrella and a waterproof cloak are essentials; and whoever wishes to become what Mr. Mantalini expressively terms "a dem'd moist unpleasant body" had better go to Bergen and spend a week without them.

The fish-market, situated at the head of the merchant harbour, is one of the most interesting sights of this ancient city; and those who wish to see it to advantage ought to go about seven in

the morning when the fishing-boats come throng-
ing in with their scaly freight. The fish are
brought to market alive by a very ingenious
contrivance. Each fishing-boat tows along by a
cord attached to it a small, flat-bottomed, boat-
shaped receptacle, in which the fish are placed;
and the sides of this are pierced with holes,
through which the water flows freely, so that it is
almost entirely submerged as it is towed astern
with its living burden. In going to the fish-
market, we passed in front of the lofty white warehouses once the property of the merchants of the
Hanseatic League. A perfect fleet of fishing-boats,
ranged in two tiers, lay alongside the quay in
front of them; and, close to its edge. stands a row
of tall, upright, mast-like posts painted green,
with long black poles slung across them, one end
of which admits of being lowered into vessels
lying alongside the wharf, when, by hauling on the
other end, any article attached may be easily
raised and deposited on the quay. It was curious
to see these rude and ancient substitutes for the
crane and windlass still standing in the middle of
the nineteenth century.

On reaching the fish-market we found ourselves in the midst of a perfect babel of tongues,

bargaining, chaffering, and abusing, with a volu-
bility and energy worthy of Billingsgate. The
market and its neighbourhood offer great attractions to the artist. Several of the adjacent
buildings are curious and characteristic, many
fine studies of costume present themselves, and
some of the picturesque Loffoden galleys are
generally moored close by. These vessels sometimes bring to Bergen a cargo of wood piled up
till it is almost half-mast high, and are said
occasionally to take back with them a cargo of
coffins, using them as packing-cases during their
homeward voyage. From the fish-market we
continued our walk until we reached the shores
of an inland lake connected with the harbour by
a narrow canal, and surrounded by pleasant walks
and wooded slopes, with the villas of the Bergen
merchants peeping out from among the foliage.
It is a beautiful spot, and presents a charming
combination of wood and water; yet that large
yellow building which arrests the eye by its size
and beauty of situation calls up saddening associations, for it is the Hospital for Lepers. leprosy
being a disease, unfortunately. still prevalent in
Bergen.

On our way back we visited several shops, in

particular that of Mr. F. Berger, a bookseller, whose shop is situated not far from the cathedral. He is an accomplished linguist, speaking English and German with fluency. We found him very civil and attentive, and were introduced by him to the Bergen Athenæum, where we saw *Punch*, the *Examiner*, and the *Illustrated News*. Strangers introduced by a member enter their names in a book kept for that purpose, and are then entitled to the use of the rooms for a fortnight free of expense. Afterwards we went to the Bergen Museum, which contains a highly interesting collection of articles connected with the natural history, antiquities, and fine arts of Norway. We saw a splendid specimen of that noblest of the falcon tribe, the gerfalcon of Norway, and of the capercailzie, male and female, a fine lynx, the skeletons of several large bears, and a great variety of fishes, reptiles, and minerals. There is also a curious collection of ancient Norsk swords, axes, and armour, and specimens of wood and stone covered with runic characters. Several pairs of the snow-shoes or skates in common use were pointed out to us. These are narrow flat pieces of wood, about eight feet in length, tapering at each end, with a strap of leather to attach them

to the feet, and the face next the ground grooved.
Those used by the Laplanders are of unequal
length, and the shorter of the two is covered with
reindeer-skin, in order to enable them to climb
steep acclivities. We were shown a beautifully-
carved wooden bedstead of the end of the sixteenth
or beginning of the seventeenth century, said to
have belonged to a daughter of a king of Scotland.
Whether this legend be true or no, it is a most
elaborate and delicate piece of carving. The
Museum contains many pictures, most of them
very bad, though often having great names
attached. Among them we observed a portrait
of Jacob Jacobson Drachenberg, the Old Parr of
Norway, who lived 150 years; a good landscape
by Professor Dahl of Dresden; a smaller Italian
scene by the same artist, and a very noble outline
drawing of a Pietà, worthy of the best days of
Italian art. But the two most interesting pictures
are by Jansen, a Norwegian priest, a pupil of the
school of Dusseldorf; the one representing the fair
Ingeborge, the heroine of Frithiofs Saga, with a
falcon on her wrist, looking out upon the sea,
awaiting the return of her hero lover. The drawing is good, the face beautiful, and, with the
exception of a little hardness, the colouring agree-

able. The other picture represents one of the
Norwegian Vikings carrying off a Greek captive.
The warm voluptuous character of southern beauty
is well expressed, and contrasts strongly with the
bright complexion and fair hair and beard of the
northern warrior. The drawing of the left arm of
the young Greek is, however, bad and feeble. We
were informed that a new building is shortly to be
erected for the better accommodation and arrangement of the curiosities of the Museum.

On a subsequent day we went to see the first
exhibition of the Prize Pictures (chiefly by native
artists) of the Bergen Art Union. This association
was then quite in its infancy, having subsisted for
a single year only ; the annual subscription is two
dollars, and the largest sum as yet given for a
picture has been 100 dollars. The prizes are
decided, as with us, by ballot, and the names of
the prize-holders are affixed to the pictures they
have won. Several of the landscapes by native
artists showed great technical proficiency, and an
attentive and loving study of nature ; and we have
no doubt that many of them would bring in this
country twice the sum given for them in Norway.
The exhibition did not contain a single specimen
of historical painting, but consisted entirely of

landscapes and *tableaux de genre*. Among the native artists we particularly noticed the landscapes of Mortens Müller and Nils Müller, and of Ecker, a Norwegian long resident in the island of Madeira. There was also a very promising picture, "Children at play," by Bergslien, a Norsk peasant youth, whose genius for painting induced some benevolent individuals to send him to study at Dusseldorf, which appears to be the favourite school with Norwegian artists.

On Sunday we attended afternoon service in the Cathedral, which has no external beauty to boast of, and, internally, is probably the ugliest church in Europe. It is a large building, but there were not above thirty persons present during the service, which lasted for about an hour. The officiating clergyman was a fine-looking middle-aged man, and, like the Lutheran clergy in general, wore a black gown and Geneva ruff. He possessed a splendid voice, and read his sermon with great solemnity and effect. The interior of the Cathedral is as white as whitewash and paint can make it. There is a long and lofty nave with a wooden roof totally devoid of mouldings or ornaments of any kind. This is divided from a low aisle by three huge, ugly, octagonal pillars, with the shafts whitewashed and the capitals painted black. The aisle is partially filled up by several tiers of pews, exactly like the boxes in an opera-house, and the central pew opposite the pulpit has red curtains attached to it. The pulpit is a frightful wooden structure some thirty feet high, which rises in successive stories and rests against the centre of the wall of the nave, while below, it is supported upon the head of a single unfortunate wooden angel, who seems quite inadequate to sustain such a burden. Above the altar rises a huge wooden canopy, in one compartment of which is a painting of the Lord's Supper, surmounted by a circular pediment, above which is a crucifixion, the whole towering up almost to the roof in elaborate and unmitigated ugliness. In front of the altar, and within the altar railings, are two large brass lamps suspended from the ceiling by black rods, ornamented with brass bells at regular intervals; and between these lamps hangs a colossal figure with gilt wings and scanty drapery, resembling a figurante let down from the flies of an opera-house rather than a respectable and orthodox angel which we supposed it to represent. This figure may be pulled up and lowered down by a ring attached to it, an operation which we witnessed during the baptismal service, the water being contained in a basin placed upon a wreath held by the outstretched hand of the suspended angel. Facing the altar, at the opposite extremity of the nave, is a large and powerful organ with a fine full tone. It was very well played. Its exterior, however, is in perfect keeping with the general hideousness which characterises the interior of this extraordinary building. There are three parish churches in Bergen -the Cathedral, the Kors Kirke, and the New Church. After leaving the Cathedral we visited the last of these, arriving just at the termination of the service. The congregation was far more numerous than in the Cathedral, the passages were strewed with twigs of juniper, and paint and whitewash seemed in as great favour as in the Metropolitan church.

On our way back, we spent some time in searching out an apothecary, in order to get some medicine for one of our party who had been taken ill at Bergen. We found that there were two compounders of drugs, the one known by the sign of a swan, and the other by that of a lion, suspended over their doors. We patronised the latter; and, in spite of his formidable designation of " Löve Aphothek," found him civil and attentive, and able to speak a little English. Besides the two

apothecaries, the health of the population is watched
over by sixteen doctors; and a diploma from the
University of Christiania is absolutely necessary
before any one is allowed to practise. Even a
Swedish diploma will not do. None but Norwegians,
or at least those holding a Norwegian degree, are permitted to kill or cure their fellow-citizens in Bergen.

Next day the rainy monotony of the weather
was diversified by a violent thunderstorm, and
we were confined to our cabin finishing sketches,
writing up journals, and making arrangements for
our departure. The weather was somewhat better
next morning, and at eleven o'clock we started
on our homeward voyage to Lerwick by the mouth
of the Kors Fiord, which opens into the German
Ocean about eighteen miles from Bergen. The sky
was comparatively clear, and the views of the old
Norwegian capital as we sailed away were varied
and beautiful. From a point about a mile to the
north of King Haco's castle the appearance of the
city is very picturesque. The quaint irregular
buildings of the old fortress rising from the
sheltered waters of the merchant harbour form a
noble foreground, while the twin spires of the
German Church and those of the Cathedral and
Kors Kirke group finely around them. Farther

back is the tall white range of the Hanseatic
warehouses; and, along each side and at the head
of the merchant harbour, a perfect forest of masts;
while facing the old castle on the other side of the
bay are the white walls and spire of the New
Church, the slopes behind it covered by groups of
picturesque and brightly-painted wooden houses,
above which frowns the ancient fortress of
Fredericksburg. But, perhaps, the most complete
of all the sea views of Bergen is that obtained from a
point a short distance beyond the extremity of the
long peninsula which divides the two bays around
which the town extends. This view shows more of
the city than any other, and its various buildings
form most picturesque and charming combinations.
Not far from Bergen, and looking almost like a
long suburb, is the pretty village of Nyhavn, built
close to the sea along the foot of a range of steep
hills. It is a favourite summer resort of the
Bergenese.

On our way to the mouth of the Kors Fiord, and
while sailing through its narrow and winding
reaches, we passed many a charming villa, many a
sequestered parsonage house and church peeping
out from thick foliage, and many a sheltered bay
and fishing village built along the beach. Among

the prettiest of these villages are Strudhavn, Stargen, Bradholm and Klokervik; but, although every spot of fertile ground is taken advantage of, here. as on the banks of the Hardanger, the general characteristic of the shores of the fiord is extreme barrenness. At five o'clock we reached the beacon on Marsten Island off the mouth of the Kors Fiord, where we parted with our venerable pilot. They apparently provide for their old men in Norway by teaching them to say "'Bout ship!" and then making pilots of them. This old man seemed still more aged than our invaluable Palinurus on the Moranger Fiord. He had lost most of his teeth, and his hair and whiskers were quite white. Pilotage for our small vessel during our short visit to Norway cost us considerably more than £1 per day; and we had a learned discussion in the cabin one forenoon whether the Norsk word *lootz* (pilot) might not be derived from the Hindoo *loot*, meaning booty or plunder: a question which we leave to the decision of more accomplished philologists.

After a stormy voyage of fifty-one hours against a head wind and a heavy sea, we arrived safely at Lerwick, from which we had taken our departure just a fortnight before. Of this period nearly four days were occupied in the voyage out and home, and ten days were spent in Norway, which serves to show how easily, and in how short a time, some of the finest scenery in Europe may be reached and enjoyed by those who do not suffer from sea-sickness, or object to the confinement and limited accommodation of a small vessel.

A LOFFODEN FISHING BOAT.

SHETLAND MILL.

CHAPTER VI

A YACHT CRUISE AMONG THE SHETLAND ISLANDS

THE barren and distant Shetland Islands, in spite of the rapid tides and stormy seas which surround them, and of the total absence of all the softer features of scenery, present many attractions to the adventurous yachtsman. They abound in safe harbours, and their cliffs and headlands are unequalled among the British Isles. They also contain numerous remains of ancient forts or Burghs, whose age and uses are now matter for conjecture, and about whose builders as little is certainly known as about those of the pyramids of Egypt, or the round towers of Ireland. Rude

Scandinavian instruments of husbandry, and picturesque inefficient old mills, are still in common use, and many Norse expressions yet linger in the ordinary speech of the islanders. The men, by their universal preference of a sea-faring life, and contempt for agriculture, show themselves the true descendants of those old Vikings whose war galleys were, for three centuries, the terror of every coast in Europe ; while the women not only knit those stockings, shawls, and veils, whose softness and warmth have become proverbial, but also cut and carry turf, and perform all the agricultural operations reserved in most other countries for the ruder and stronger sex. Inns are scarce, but the hospitality universally practised by the clergy, gentry, and farmers amply supplies their place ; and the capital trout-fishing in the numerous fresh-water lochs, and at the head of the voes or narrow inlets of the sea, offers a strong temptation to the enterprising sportsman.

On our return from a voyage to Norway, we spent a fortnight among these rugged and treeless islands, which we now propose describing, first asking the reader to glance for a moment at their early history, which possesses many elements of romantic interest. In the ninth century a Norwegian prince, Harald Harfagr. or the fair-haired, became enamoured of the beautiful Princess Gida, the loveliest maiden in Europe. He proposed to marry her, but the proud beauty rejected his suit. "You are not yet sufficiently renowned; reduce all Norway under your sway, and then I may listen to your love," was Gida's reply to her fair-haired adorer. Harald accepted the task, and vowed to suffer his golden locks to grow until he had conquered the kingdom and won the bride. He did both; but many of the petty princes of Norway whom he had driven from their country took refuge with their warlike followers in the Orkney and Shetland Islands, and thence made repeated and desolating descents upon the coasts of Norway. Summer after summer these were renewed, until at length Harald was roused to vengeance, assembled a powerful armament, sailed to Orkney and Shetland, and reduced both groups of islands under his sway. He then conferred them as an earldom upon Ronald, Count of Merea, who resigned the donation in favour of his brother Sigurd, first Jarl or Earl of Orkney. For several hundred years the Orkney and Shetland Islands remained under the dominion of the

Norwegian crown; but in the thirteenth century they were transferred from the Government of Norway to that of Scotland, in security of 58,000 florins, part of the dowry of Margaret, daughter of the King of Norway, on her marriage to James the Third. In the previous century, Henry Sinclair, a Scotchman, who had by marriage acquired the best right to the Earldom of Orkney, received an investiture of it from the King of Denmark, then also monarch of Norway, and he and his descendants held the earldom for nearly one hundred years. But after the islands had been pledged to the Scottish crown, Lord Sinclair gave up his right in them to James the Third, in exchange for the castle and lands of Ravenscraig in Scotland, upon which the king by a formal statute annexed them to the Crown. Soon after this annexation, the Norsk language began to fall into desuetude; but in their manners, domestic habits, language, and appearance, the Shetlanders still bear traces of their Scandinavian descent. The single - stilted plough, and the rude corn-mills, now as of old in use, and the tusker, quern, and cassie, are genuine Scandinavian implements of husbandry, and nearly two hundred words of Norsk origin are still employed by the inhabitants. But though the

N

Northmen have stamped the impress of their race indelibly on the character and habits of the Shetlanders, traces of earlier and more civilised conquerors are still to be found in many of the islands. Coins of Vespasian, Galba, Ælius Cæsar, and Trajan have been dug up in various places. In the year 84 of our era, Agricola visited the Orkneys during his circumnavigation of Great Britain; and in the fourth century Theodosius also did so, and most probably extended his voyage to Shetland. As to the original inhabitants, they appear to have been a Pictish tribe of Celtic origin about whom little is known; but through the darkness and uncertainty which shroud these remote ages, we may discern three important epochs in the early history of these islands. First, Agricola's visit when they were inhabited by a Celtic race; second, their conquest A.D. 368 by Theodosius, at which period they were the strongholds of Saxon pirates who made wasting descents upon the British coasts; and third, the sixth century, when they fell into the hands of the Scandinavians, the ancestors of the present inhabitants.

But to pass from the days of war-galleys and vikings, when piracy was considered a gentlemanly

and respectable occupation, to our present state of
morality and civilisation, when we start on a
cruise to cure dyspepsia or dispel ennui—it was a
beautiful autumn morning when we came in sight
of the majestic cliffs of Sumburgh and Fitful Head
immortalised by Sir Walter Scott in the *Pirate*.
Soon after, we passed through the Roost of Sumburgh, where we were terribly tossed about until
we got beyond its stormy influence. Roost or
Roust, a word of frequent occurrence among the
Orkney and Shetland Islands, is a term of Scandinavian origin, meaning a strong tumultuous current
caused by the meeting of rapid tides. Sumburgh
Roost, even in calm weather, has the appearance of
a turbulent tide stream two or three miles wide
extending a short distance from the headland
which gives it its name, and then gradually
dwindling to a long dark line stretching away
towards Fair Isle. At the commencement of the
flood in the Roost, the tide flows to the eastward
until it passes the head ; it there meets a southern
tide, which causes a divergence, first to the south-
east, and then to the south. At high water there
is a short cessation, called the " still," after which
the ebb begins, setting first north-west and then
north, until the recommencement of the flood. A

sloop has been becalmed for five days between Sumburgh Head and Fitful Head, which are only three miles distant from each other, without being able to pass either, in consequence of one current impelling her into the eastern, and an opposing one into the western sea.

Viewed from the sea, Fitful Head presents a somewhat rounded and bluff outline, terminating in an almost perpendicular cliff, from which there is a gradual slope inland to the low ground that surrounds Quendal Bay. Beyond this, the land again rises, till it culminates in Sumburgh Head, which presents to the sea a sheer wall of rock, on the highest point of which gleam the white walls and tower of a lighthouse, to warn the mariner against the dangers of the stormy roost. Below the precipice are the Links of Sumburgh, famous in Shetland history as the scene of a desperate battle fought many centuries ago between the Shetlanders and the men of Lewis. The feud between them had been of long standing, and many a combat and wasting foray had embittered their mutual animosity, which is said to have originated in the following circumstance. In the middle of the thirteenth century, when King Haco of Norway, to whom Shetland then belonged, made his famous expedition against Scotland, which terminated in his defeat at the battle of Largs, he detached a body of troops to hold the island of Lewis in check. These troops impoverished the islanders by grinding exactions, and exasperated them by

FLUGGA STACK, NORTHMOST LIGHTHOUSE IN BRITISH ISLES.

repeated acts of atrocity, until at length a plot was formed for cutting off the hated invaders. The lord of the island ordered the croistarich[1] to be constructed, the ritual fire to be kindled, and a goat to be slain. The extremities of a wooden cross were then lighted, and the flames quenched in the blood of the slain animal. This emblem of

[1] This word is expressive of a popular signal, being derived from *crois*, a cross, and *tara*, a multitude.

fire and sword was then despatched by a swift
messenger throughout the island with the terrible
mandate, "Let every man slay his guest." The
messenger sped to the nearest hamlet, and there
presented the token which bound him who received
it, on pain of being pronounced infamous, to obey
his chieftain's command to slay his guest, and
afterwards, in his turn, speed onward as bearer of
the bloody token to the next hamlet, where a
similar tragedy was enacted, and thus all Haco's
warriors fell beneath the steel of the islanders.
But even this bloody vengeance did not satiate the
hatred of the Lewismen, who transmitted their
hostility to Shetland from generation to generation,
and even subsequently to the union of the islands
with the Scottish Crown, used to make desolating
descents upon their shores. Their last battle with
the Shetlanders is said to have been fought on the
Links of Sumburgh, where the islanders, drawn up
in battle array under the leadership of one of the
Sinclairs of Brow, awaited the assault of their
invaders. The combat that took place was of the
most desperate character, and attended with great
slaughter on both sides; but at length victory
declared for the Shetlanders, and not a single Lewis-
man returned to tell the fate of his companions.

The vanquished were buried in heaps where they fell, and mounds of sand piled above their graves. These were long afterwards swept away during a violent storm, which laid bare quantities of human bones thrown indiscriminately together.

After passing Sumburgh Head, we entered the Sound of Mousa, as the arm of the sea which separates the island of that name from the Mainland is called. The most interesting relic of antiquity in the whole Shetland group is the curious old tower termed the Burgh of Mousa. It occupies a site close to the sea, is circular in shape, and measures about fifty feet in diameter at the base, by forty-two feet in height, swelling out from the foundation, and then getting smaller towards the top. The stones of which it is built are of medium size, carefully laid together, but without any cement. The doorway is low, and leads to a narrow passage which can only be explored by creeping on the hands and knees. This traversed admits to an open area inclosed by the walls of the building, which are of the great thickness of fifteen feet. The diameter of the open space is twenty-one feet. The walls of this singular structure are hollow, and pierced by several rows of small chambers, to which access is afforded by means of a winding stone

staircase three feet in width. In fact, the shell of
the building consists of two concentric walls, one
about five feet, and the other about four and a
half in thickness, while a space of nearly similar
extent is occupied by a number of small low
chambers. The roofs of the lowest range of
apartments form the floors of those above ; and, in
this way, no less than seven tiers of chambers wind
round the building. The Burgh is supposed by
some to have been intended as a place of refuge
from the attacks of the pirates by whom these
islands were once devastated, and these small dark
chambers, protected by thick strong walls, are
believed to have been constructed as places of
shelter for the women and children, and also as
repositories for grain and other valuables. This,
however, is mere conjecture; for the origin, intention, and history of the Burgh of Mousa are alike a
mystery which the researches of the subtlest anti-
quarians have hitherto failed to penetrate.

Strangely enough, the Nuraghe of Sardinia
present in their external aspect a striking resemblance to the Burgh of Mousa. These Nuraghe
are round towers generally built on the summit of
hillocks or artificial mounds commanding an
extensive view over the surrounding country. In

form they are truncated cones varying from 30 to
60 feet in height, and from 100 to 300 feet in
circumference at the base, and no fewer than 3000
of them, in a more or less ruinous state, are said to
be still existing in the island of Sardinia.   Their
walls are composed of rough masses of stone,
built in regular horizontal layers, and gradually
diminishing in size to the summit.   In most
instances they show no marks of the chisel, but in
some cases the stones appear to have been rudely
worked by the hammer, though not exactly squared.
The interior of these Nuraghe, however, is very
different from that of the Burgh of Mousa.   It is
thus described by a recent traveller.[1]   "The
interior is almost invariably divided into two
domed chambers one above the other; the lowest
averaging from 15 to 20 feet in diameter, and from
20 to 25 in height.   Access to the upper chamber
is gained by a spiral ramp or rude steps between
the internal and external walls.   These are continued to the summit of the tower, which is
generally supposed to have formed a platform, but
scarcely any of the Nuraghe now present a perfect
apex.   On the ground-floor there are generally
found from two to four cells worked in the solid

[1] Forrester, *Rambles in Corsica and Sardinia.*

masonry of the base of the cone." Afterwards, the entrance to one of these Nuraghe is described. " The entrance was so low that we were obliged to stoop almost to our knees in passing through it. A lintel, consisting of a single stone some two tons weight, was supported by the protruding jambs. No light being admitted to the chamber but by a low passage through the double walls, it was gloomy enough." It will thus be evident that though the position, external appearance, double walls, low narrow entrance, and cells excavated in the solid masonry of the base of these Nuraghe bear a striking analogy to the Shetland Burghs, yet the arrangement of their interior into two great domed chambers presents a marked contrast to the seven tiers or nests of apartments that wind between the concentric walls of the Burgh of Mousa. The origin, history, and purposes of these Nuraghe have excited quite as much interest among Sardinian antiquaries as those of the Burghs have done among ourselves; and La Marmora and Father Bresciani, the most recent and best authorities, agree in supposing them to have been intended to serve as religious edifices or tombs for the dead, and in imputing to them an eastern origin, probably Canaanitish or Phœnician.

On emerging from the Sound of Mousa, we came
in sight of two tall and precipitous cliffs, called the
Bard of Bressay and Noss Head. The former is
pierced by a singular cavern, through which a boat
may be rowed from sea to sea. We sailed past yet

NOSS HEAD.

another headland, called the Ord of Bressay, and
then—leaving it behind us and rounding a low
point—entered the landlocked Sound of Bressay,
the first port we made in the Shetland Islands. This
Sound, separating the island of Bressay from that
of the Mainland, forms one of the finest harbours
in Great Britain, and is a favourite rendezvous of
vessels bound for the whale-fishery in the northern

seas. On the western sides of the harbour lies the little town of Lerwick, the capital of Shetland. It contains about 3000 inhabitants, and, viewed from the Sound, its appearance is both picturesque and peculiar, the gables of most of the houses facing the water, while numberless piers and jetties project into the harbour, whose sheltered waters stretch north and south for nearly four miles with an average breadth of about a mile. The town is built along a peninsula, whose northern extremity is crowned by a fort commanding a fine view of the harbour and of the opposite island of Bressay, green with rich pasture fields, and famous throughout Shetland for its milk and butter. This fort was erected in 1665, at a cost of £28,000, and, during the Dutch war of that period, was garrisoned by Colonel William Sinclair and 300 men for three years. At the commencement of the eighteenth century it was attacked and burnt by a Dutch frigate, but was repaired in 1781 and named Fort Charlotte; at present a sergeant and a few artillery-men are its only garrison. There is a good deal of bustle and gaiety in Lerwick during two periods of the year: first in spring, when a great number of whaling vessels come into the harbour to get manned; and afterwards, in August and September,

when French and Dutch men-of-war often come in
to look after their boats engaged in the fisheries
along these coasts. Several Dutch fishing smacks
were anchored close to where we lay; they are
clumsy but picturesque-looking craft, carrying a
tall mast and heavy square-sail, while a smaller
mast, on which a shoulder-of-mutton sail is spread,
is stepped close to the stern of the vessel. The
skippers of these boats were strange-looking animals,
fat and unctuous, dressed in thick woollen jerseys
and most voluminous breeches. It was amusing to
watch them scrambling over the lofty sides of their
vessels from the low shore boats in which they had
been pulled off from the town. These Dutch
fishing smacks carry no boats of their own, and keep
the sea in all weathers.

A dangerous rock lies in the northern entrance
to Bressay Sound. It is known as the Unicorn, a
name which it acquired from the following
catastrophe. When the profligate Earl of Bothwell
became an outlaw and a pirate, he captured several
of the vessels belonging to these islands; and, in
order to protect them against his attacks, the
Scottish Government despatched two ships of war
in pursuit of him. One of these vessels, commanded
by Kirkaldy of Grange, and named the *Unicorn*,

got close to the ship of the pirate earl near Bressay
Sound. Kirkaldy's steersman was ignorant of the
coast, but his gallant commander crowded all sail
in pursuit, and the *Unicorn* was rapidly gaining on
her foe, when the skilful pilot who held the helm
of Bothwell's vessel steered her so as just to graze
the hidden danger. Kirkaldy followed close in her
wake; but his ship, less adroitly handled, struck
upon the rock, and soon went to pieces, and ever
since that time the fatal reef has borne the name
of his luckless vessel.

Our first object, on landing at Lerwick, was to
find out the Post Office, which stands in
Commercial Street, a long narrow thoroughfare,
paved with flat stones, which traverses the whole
length of the town. We received our letters from
an amusing and eccentric public functionary, who,
besides acting as clerk to the Postmaster, binds
books, teaches elocution and dancing, and takes
photographs. Afterwards we walked to Cleikum
Loch, about a mile and a half from Lerwick, where,
upon an island connected with the shore by a
narrow causeway, are the ruins of an ancient
Pictish fort supposed to have been similar to that
on the island of Mousa. The island in the loch,
covered with gray masses of time-worn stones, and

backed by brown and bleak hills, forms a fine
subject for the pencil. Next day we made an
excursion to the Lochs of Tingwall, about five
miles distant from Lerwick. The road traverses a
hilly district, and, near the town, every hill-side is
scarped and broken up by the operations of the
turf-cutters. We met numbers of them going to
and returning from the peat moss. They were all
women, and carried the peats on their backs in
baskets exactly like inverted beehives. Many of
them, as they trudged along the road, bending
under their loads, were engaged in knitting ;
several were good-looking and picturesquely
dressed ; and an artist might easily have formed
from among them an excellent foreground group
for a picture of turf-cutting in Shetland. The
Lochs of Tingwall fill up a hollow, with steep hills
on one side and gentler slopes on the other. They
abound in fish ; but, to fish them successfully, one
must either wade very deep or procure a boat, as
there is a great extent of shallow water along their
margins. These lochs derive their name from a
small green holm or island close to the shore of the
upper loch, where courts of law used formerly to
hold their meetings, from which it was termed—
like similar places of convocation in Iceland and

elsewhere—Thingvalla, now corrupted into Tingwall. The Court of Tingwall was under the
jurisdiction of the Foude or Governor, and the laws
relating to particular districts were framed at the
law tings or assemblies of the householders of these
districts. Under the Norwegian rule, there were
five of these tings in Shetland, and, under the
Scottish dominion, ten, and they continued to exist
in Orkney and Shetland until 1670. Lord
Dufferin, in his delightful *Yacht Cruise to
Iceland*, etc., gives an animated description of his
visit to a Thingvalla in that island ; there, the ting
was held on a rock, surrounded on all sides by a
profound chasm passable only at one place, where
a narrow ledge of rock connected it with the
surrounding plain. On this rock the Icelandic
householders held their meetings, just as those of
Shetland did on the green holm. The ledge
leading to the rock, and the causeway to the holm,
were guarded by armed men during the meetings
of the tings ; but, in Shetland, if a criminal could
break through the guards and reach the ancient
Church of Tingwall without being captured, he
was permitted to escape unpunished. There is
still to be seen, in the churchyard near the
ruins of the old church, a stone almost covered

with moss and lichens, and bearing the following inscription—

Here lies an honest man, Thomas Boyne, sometimes Foude of Tingwall.

After fishing the lochs with tolerable success, we walked to the fine old ruin of Scalloway Castle, passing on the way a tall upright monumental stone, which, according to one tradition, is said to have been erected to commemorate the death of a Danish general who was there slain while endeavouring to reduce the Norwegian colonists to submission. Another legend, however, affirms that it is a memorial stone raised to mark the spot where a son of an ancient Earl of Orkney was murdered by his father's orders. This youth, having incurred his father's displeasure, fled to a stronghold on an island in a loch in the district of Tingwall; upon which the incensed earl sent a party of retainers from Orkney with peremptory instructions to bring back the fugitive dead or alive. They came up with the unfortunate noble-man in the valley of Tingwall, and immediately attacked and killed him, after which they cut off his head, and, on their return to Orkney, laid the ghastly token at his father's feet to show how faithfully his commands had been obeyed. But

they met with a retribution they little anticipated.
In a sudden revulsion of feeling, the stern earl
wept over the head of his son, ordered his
murderers to instant execution, and afterwards
erected this stone on the spot where he fell.

Scalloway Castle was built in the year 1600
by the infamous Earl Patrick, the tyrant of the
Orkney and Shetland Islands, whose crimes at
length brought him to the scaffold. It is a square
tower three stories in height, with large windows,
and on the summit of each angle of the building
is a small round turret. It is now a mere shell,
and the interior is allowed to remain in a filthy
state, no effort whatever being made to preserve
this fine old ruin from dirt and decay. In order to
defray the expense incurred in building Scalloway
Castle, Earl Patrick imposed heavy taxes upon
the Shetlanders, by whom he was deservedly and
universally hated. On completing the castle, he
applied to a Mr. Pitcairn, minister of Northmavine,
a bold and witty man, for an inscription to be
placed over the gateway of his new abode, and
received the following verse of Scripture in answer
—"That house which is built upon a rock shall
stand, but built upon the sand it will fall." Dis-
guising his resentment at the implied censure, the

earl quietly remarked, "My father's house was built upon the sand, its foundations are already giving way, and it will fall; but Scalloway Castle is founded on a rock and will stand." He then desired Mr. Pitcairn to turn the verse he had selected into a Latin distich, which he caused to be sculptured over the principal gateway of the castle, where traces of the letters are still visible.

Nearly a third of the adult male population of the Shetland Isles are occupied in seafaring pursuits; from 1000 to 1500 engage annually in the Greenland whale and seal fisheries, and as many go southward to serve as sailors in merchant vessels. On this account it is often very difficult to get agricultural labourers even at high wages, and they sometimes require to be imported from the county of Caithness. The boats almost universally used by the Shetland fishermen are Norwegian skiffs, small fragile craft carrying a large lug-sail, in the management of which they are very expert. The smaller skiffs, those from ten to twelve feet keel, are brought over from Norway complete, while the larger ones, from twelve to twenty-two feet keel, are first put together in Norway, then taken to pieces, and sent over to

Shetland in planks numbered and assorted, so that they can be easily put together again.

Some curious superstitions still exist among the Shetlanders; one of the most singular relating to the extraordinary powers of those who belong to masonic fraternities. The fishermen will scarcely go to sea on the day when a masonic lodge meets, and the common people very generally believe that freemasons have the power of discovering lost and stolen goods. A woman recently walked fifteen miles to inquire of a gentleman belonging to a lodge of freemasons what had become of an old petticoat which she had lost; and, on another occasion, a young man came from a considerable distance for the purpose of ascertaining from a freemason who was the real father of an illegitimate child which had been unjustly fathered upon him. Many curious anecdotes are told of the discoveries made by Shetland freemasons ingeniously taking advantage of the popular belief in their extraordinary powers. Thus a poor labourer had been robbed of his little hard-earned stock of money, and applied to a freemason for assistance in discovering the robber and getting back his hoard. The freemason directed him to give public notice of his application to him, and to advertise on the

church door that the money must be brought back
to a place specified in the neighbourhood of the
house from which it had been taken by a certain
day, at the same time promising that no one would
be on the look-out to observe who restored it ;
and such was the influence of the popular belief,
that the stolen money was actually returned on
the appointed day.

Before leaving Lerwick Harbour, we spent a day
very pleasantly in an excursion to Noss Head, the
loftiest cliff in these islands. We landed on the
island of Bressay, which is about two miles wide,
walked across it, were ferried over the narrow
channel which divides the islands of Noss and
Bressay, and then commenced the ascent of the
steep grassy slope that leads to the summit of the
magnificent headland, so familiar an object to all
who visit these stormy seas. In three-quarters of
an hour we reached the verge of the cliff, where,
upon lying down and peering cautiously over, we
could see the ocean washing the foot of the
precipice 700 feet beneath ; while countless flocks
of sea-birds were wheeling and screaming in mid-
air, or dotting every ledge and projection on the
face of the rock like spots of snow. The view
from the summit was magnificent. To the north-

ward, divided by many a winding sound, and
indented by many a voe, island after island
stretched away farther than the eye could reach.
Eastward lay an unbroken expanse of sea. To the
westward were the green slopes of Noss, the island
and Ward Hill of Bressay, and the town of Lerwick;
while far to the south rose the bold cliffs of Sumburgh and Fitful Head. After enjoying for some
time this noble and varied prospect, we proceeded
to visit the Cradle of Noss, which is a movable
wooden chair or box attached to two slender ropes,
spanning a tremendous chasm which separates the
Holm of Noss from the main island. The Holm of
Noss, thus rudely joined to the larger island of the
same name, rises abruptly 160 feet above the sea,
and is girt in on all sides by inaccessible precipices.
It is very small—about 500 feet long by 170 wide,
but its surface is flat, and covered with tolerable
pasturage. The chasm across which the cradle
extends is sixty-five feet wide; the sea below
thirty feet deep. The farmer on Noss breeds a
great number of Shetland ponies, and some of
those we saw on the island were exceedingly handsome. There are several fresh-water lochs on
Bressay, in one of which there are fine pink-fleshed
trout. They are, however, very shy, and we only

succeeded in enticing two good ones into our basket.

Next day, under the guidance of a gentleman to whose unwearied kindness and attention we were deeply indebted during our stay, we set out on a walk to the ruined Burgh of Brindister, about five miles to the south-west of Lerwick. On our way we passed the pretty bay of Gulbervik, where there is a good deal of cultivation, chiefly on what is termed the run-rig system. There is no rotation of crops practised in Shetland, and one of the farmers will often take five successive crops of corn from the same field. Another wasteful and injurious custom is also prevalent : the turf is cut away from the tops of the hills, and mixed with the corn-fields on the lower and more sheltered slopes, in order to improve their soil, and in this way any agricultural value which these uplands may once have possessed is destroyed for a long term of years. After a pleasant walk of an hour and a half we reached the ruined Burgh, picturesquely placed on the verge of a precipice rising 100 feet above the sea which washes its base. The low massive doorway faces westward, and scarcely a yard of green sward intervenes between it and the edge of the precipice. The walls of the ancient

tower still rise twelve feet above the ground, gray,
time-worn, and overgrown with lichens. On passing through the doorway, you enter a dark passage
or gallery three feet square, extending for about
thirty feet into the interior of the building; and a
short distance beyond the entrance, a narrow
aperture opens on the right of the passage, just
wide enough to admit the body of a man of
ordinary size. Into this one of our party, a
zealous antiquarian, who had provided himself
with a torch, contrived to crawl; and, after
wriggling about for some time, was lost to view in
the darkness. A few minutes afterwards, we saw
a head begrimed with dust emerge from the opening, followed by the shoulders belonging to it; but
having got thus far, the head and shoulders
remained stationary; so that, after having satisfied
ourselves that the dusty apparition was our friend
who had shortly before disappeared, and not a
Pictish Troll come to assault the invaders of his
privacy, we promptly laid hold of him, and by a
vigorous pull hauled him out of the passage, and
then into the open air, where his heated visage and
dusty garments provoked a general laugh. He
had, however, succeeded in reaching the penetralia
of the ancient Burgh; for, after crawling through

the narrow opening in which he so nearly stuck, he came to an inner chamber of larger dimensions, apparently about eight feet in length and height, and about four feet in width, beyond which there appeared to be no possibility of penetrating. The curiosity of our antiquarian friend being thus fully satisfied, we bade farewell to the Burgh of Brindister, whose gray stones have looked out from their wave-washed precipice, over the waste of waters, for more than a thousand years ; and, could they but find a tongue, might tell many a strange and thrilling tale of the warships of Theodosius, manned by the all-conquering Romans ; of the Saxon pirates who afterwards became the terror of the Celtic Aborigines ; of the Norsk Seakings who followed in their track ; of King Haco and his mighty expedition against Scotland ; and many another story of " the old, old time."

We afterwards paid a visit to the interior of a Shetland cottage belonging to the tenant of a small farm in the neighbourhood. It was a thatched house, containing two tolerable rooms with scarcely any furniture, but carefully swept and scrupulously clean. The outer room had an earthen floor and a large circular stone hearth, on which a peat fire was burning brightly, while above the fire was an

iron rod with a hook attached, from which a kettle
might be suspended. The inner room contained a
box-bed and a few chairs; chimneys there were
none, the smoke escaping through apertures in the
roof. The farmer and his wife were a good-looking
couple, and, like all the Shetlanders we met, most
kind and hospitable. They gave us some good
brown bread and sweet milk, and an acid composi-
tion not at all palatable, called run milk. We had
afterwards a delightful walk back to Lerwick in a
clear mild autumn evening, and got on board our
cutter much pleased with the day's excursion.

Next morning, at ten o'clock, we sailed from
Lerwick bound for Balta Sound in the island of
Unst, the most northerly of the Shetland group.
There was a strong breeze, which freshened towards
the afternoon, so that we were obliged to shorten
sail; but, under its favouring influence, we bowled
merrily along all day, passing many a stack and
skerry,[1] many an island and voe. We took the
inner passage between Lerwick and Balta Sound,
which has the advantage of being sheltered by
islands, for the greater part of the distance, from
the swell of the sea; but which is also intricate

---

[1] *Stack* signifies a precipitous rock rising from the sea,—*Skerry* a flat
insulated rock rising above high-water mark.

and beset with rocks, so that large ships generally prefer to keep outside the islands. We, however, had two Shetlanders among our crew, who had been familiar with the navigation from boyhood, and knew every rock and roost among the islands, so that, to us, the inner passage presented no dangers. We passed the Unicorn rock formerly mentioned, and, beyond it, the Inner Voder, the Mid Voder, and the Outer Voder, as well as the long line of jagged crags, rejoicing in unpronounceable names, which together form what are termed the Stepping-stones. After running the gauntlet through these threatening reefs, we passed the island of Whalsey belonging to Mr. Bruce of Simbister, one of the richest and farthest-descended proprietors in Shetland. Simbister House is a large, plain, square building, standing on a slope above a sheltered bay. It is built almost entirely of granite, and the offices and outbuildings seem very extensive. After passing Whalsey we crossed an open expanse of sea, where we felt the full force of the heavy swell from the eastward, and were a good deal knocked about until we got under the lee of the island of Fetlar, belonging to Sir Arthur Nicholson, whose residence of Burgh Hall, with its massive round tower and strangely-grouped build-

ings, forms a conspicuous and picturesque object
from the sea. Sir Arthur Nicholson is the repre-
sentative of an old baronetage dating back to the
creation of 1629. Beyond Fetlar, we entered the
harbour of Uya Sound, as the channel between
Unst and the little island of Uya is termed. At
this point two of our party left the cutter and
landed at the little village of Garda in Unst,
intending to walk across to Balta Sound, while
the yacht should stand on for the same destination
round the eastern shore of the island. After landing they proceeded to the Loch of Belmont, about
two miles distant from the village, where very fine
trout are often caught; but, owing to the cold and
boisterous weather, they had so little success that
they determined to give up fishing and attempt to
get a sketch of Mouness Castle, one of the most
interesting remains in Shetland, situated about
four miles from the scene of their piscatorial
operations. This castle consists of a square mass
of building with round towers at two of the
opposite angles, and hanging turrets at the other
two. It was founded in 1598 by Lawrence Bruce,
from whom the two Shetland families of Simbister
and Sumburgh claim to be descended. It stands
on a headland forming the south-eastern extremity

of Unst, and over the doorway is the following inscription very beautifully carved :—

List ye to know this building Quha began ?
Lawrence the Bruce he was that worthy man ;
Quha earnestly his ayris and afspring prayis
To help and not to hurt this work alwayis.

After completing their sketches of Mouness Castle they started to walk to Balta Sound, a distance of about seven miles over a brown trackless moor. They had, however, taken the precaution of laying down their course by compass, to which they steadily kept, so that, on coming in sight of the bay, the first object that greeted their eyes was the cutter lying snugly at anchor just below where they stood. On their way they saw great numbers of snipe and large flocks of golden plover; there are no grouse in these islands, though they are plentiful among the Orkneys. They passed several sombre-looking lakes and shallow mountain burns. The largest of these lakes lies in a deep hollow about three miles from Balta Sound ; it is called Watley Loch, and is said to afford excellent sport to the angler. They reached the yacht at eight in the evening ; and, as it blew a gale during the night, they had every reason to congratulate themselves on having gained

— —

so safe an anchorage. Balta Sound is a long
narrow bay completely landlocked by the small
island of Balta, which lies across its mouth. There
is a deep-water entrance both on the north and
south sides of the island, but the first is very
narrow. Within the Sound the British navy
might securely ride at anchor, for there is not a
finer harbour on our coasts than this remote bay.
It is the first port that vessels bound to this
country from Archangel can make, and our whaling
ships have frequently recourse to it for shelter.
At present there is no lighthouse on the island of
Balta, where such a guide to the storm-tossed
mariner might often be of the greatest service,
but we were told that it was intended to erect one
as soon as possible upon its southern extremity.

Unst is one of the largest of the Shetland
Islands, measuring twelve miles in length by three
in breadth, and containing a population of 3000.
Among the hills near Balta Sound is a small
stream, remarkable for the crystal purity of its
waters, which have long enjoyed a local celebrity
for their healing powers. Those who wished to
profit by the sanative virtue of the waters were
directed to walk to the source of the stream, throw
three stones on an adjacent piece of ground, and

then drink of the waters of the spring, which, under these conditions, were supposed to ensure health to the drinker. The name of this stream is the Yelaburn, or Hielaburn, which means the water or burn of health. The hills of Crucifield, Hagdale,

STANDING STONE OF UNST.

Buness, and several other places in the neighbourhood of Balta Sound, contain the valuable mineral known as chromate of iron, first discovered by Dr. Samuel Hibbert in the beginning of the present century. It is now extensively wrought, and a steam-engine has recently been erected in connection with these mines, which belong to twenty-two different proprietors, of whom the principal are Mr. Edmonston of Buness, and Mrs.

Mowatt Cameron, Buness House. The residence of Mr. Edmonston is memorable as having been the place where the celebrated French Philosopher Biot, in 1817, carried on a series of experiments for the purpose of determining, in this high latitude, the variation in the length of the seconds pendulum; and, in the following year, he was succeeded by Captain Kater, who occupied the same station with the same purpose. For his assiduous and unremitting attention to these accomplished strangers, Mr. Edmonston received the thanks of the Royal Society of London and of the National Institute of Paris.

On the road from Balta Sound to Burra Fiord, on the other side of the islands, lies the Loch of Cliff, the largest sheet of fresh water in Shetland, and the most northerly loch in the British Isles, filling a narrow limestone valley, between rocks of gneiss and serpentine. It abounds in trout of moderate size, of which we captured six dozen in the course of a day's fishing. There are said to be not fewer than ninety fresh-water lochs in the Shetlands, most of them well stocked with trout; they generally communicate with the sea, so that in the latter end of August and month of September sea-trout frequent them in great numbers;

add to this, that the fishing is not preserved, and it must be allowed that these islands hold out great attractions to the enterprising angler. On reaching the Burra Fiord, our attention was fixed by the commanding form of the hill which rises above its eastern shore. It is called Saxafiord; and on its summit are the ruins of a tower said to have been erected by a giant named Saxa. The name of the hill signifies the watch-tower of Saxa, who seems to have been a distinguished personage in these parts, as a deep circular cavity communicating with the ocean also takes its name from him, being termed Saxa's Kettle, the giant having used it for cooking his broth.

The morning after our expedition to the Loch of Cliff rose bright and beautiful; and, favoured by a gentle breeze from the south-west, we left Balta Sound, bound for the Outer Stack, the northernmost point of Her Majesty's British dominions, and in about the same latitude as the entrance to Hudson's Bay. We had to pass through the Scaw Roost, where, though there was but little wind, we were terribly tossed about by a very heavy sea which continued during the whole of the day. Not far from the entrance to the Burra Fiord we came in sight of a lighthouse

most romantically situated upon a sharp and lofty
ridge of rocks called Flugga, with which we
narrowly escaped making too close an acquaintance. We had not succeeded in getting a
sufficient offing before the wind failed us, and the
tide, and long heavy swell, were drifting us
towards the rock, so that we had to make
vigorous use of our sweeps to get clear of it. For
some time we were very anxious about the safety
of the cutter, and it was only the most strenuous
exertions that at last enabled us to creep away
from its dangerous vicinity. A long, glassy,
rolling swell from the north-west tossed us about
all night; and, when morning broke, we found
ourselves just off the entrance to Balta Sound.
About ten o'clock, however, the wished-for breeze
sprung up. We had sailed along the whole eastern
coast of the Shetlands from Sumburgh Head to
Flugga; and now our course lay southwards for
Kirkwall, the ancient capital of the Orkney Islands.
Favoured by a fine northerly breeze, we made a
speedy run during the day, all sail set, and everything drawing. This time we passed outside the
Island of Fetlar, where may still be seen, occupying a low site near the shore, an ancient work,
which some have supposed to be the remains of a

Roman encampment constructed by the soldiers of Theodosius. To the east of Fetlar lie the dangerous rocks known to sailors as the Out Skerries, on the largest of which a lighthouse has been recently erected. Two centuries ago a richly-laden vessel,

A LAKE FORT.

the *Carmelan* of Amsterdam, freighted with three millions of guilders, struck on the Skerries and went to pieces, only four of her crew being saved from the wreck.

The sky all day was cloudless, and the atmosphere singularly clear, so that we saw the islands, as we glided swiftly past their shores, to the best advantage. At one period we had Noss Head,

Sumburgh Head, Fitful Head, and Fair Isle all in view at the same moment, though the distance between the first and last of these high lands is upwards of forty-five miles. Towards sunset the bold cliffs of Shetland had faded away to blue specks in the distance, and we watched them gradually dwindle and disappear, seeming to sink in the ocean, as the favouring breeze bore us rapidly farther and farther away.

Note.—For an account of the Mussel and Oyster Fisheries in the Shetland Islands, the latter of which have been as much exhausted as those in the Orkney Islands, as described in Chapter I. pages 11-14, see the statement in my Report of 1887, which forms Appendix B.

BRESSAY AND NOSS HEAD.

APPENDIX A

The Fisheries of Orkney.

In the beginning of July 1886 I commenced my inspection of the Fisheries in Orkney by driving from Stromness to the Bridge of Waithe, under which the waters of Loch Stenness flow into the sea in a deep strong current, through three arches, and the flood tide from the sea mingles with the waters of the loch.

Loch Stenness is a great sheet of water about 15 miles in circumference, including its upper and lower divisions. The name is sometimes applied to designate both the divisions of the loch, and sometimes it is applied only to the lower loch which communicates with the sea; while the upper loch, which is entirely fresh, is termed the Loch of Harray. The banks of these lakes, like those of all the Orcadian lakes, are bare and treeless; and the upper loch is divided from the lower by two long narrow promontories that jut out from opposite sides, and so nearly meet in the middle as to be connected by a low bridge, called the Bridge of Brogar, over which the roadway passes.

The area of the Loch of Stenness is 1792 acres, and that of the Loch of Harray 2432 acres; or, together, 4224 acres. A better idea of their great extent will be got when I state that the famous Loch Leven, in Fifeshire, which receives nearly the whole drainage of the county of Kinross, which yields an average of at least 11,000 trout per annum, the mean weight of each trout being nearly a pound, and brings a rental of £1000 a year to its fortunate possessor, has an area of only 3406 acres, or 818 acres less than Stenness and

Harray. I am quite convinced that, if these lochs were as
well protected as Loch Leven they would soon become as
productive. And it should be kept in mind that their season
commences just about the time when that on Loch Leven ends.

A deep margin of sea-weed extends for some distance above
the Bridge of Waithe into the Loch of Stenness, and on the
seaward side of the bridge there is also a thick growth of
sea-weeds. Beyond the margin of sea-weeds only inside the
Bridge of Waithe, we find a little farther on sea-weeds mixed
with fresh-water plants, and in the Loch of Harray fresh-water
plants alone. Stenness is decidedly brackish, while the water
in Harray is fresh; the former is nearly 4 miles long, with
a maximum breadth of 1½ miles ; while the latter is 4¾ miles
long, and varying in breadth from 3 furlongs to 1¾ miles.
There is no transmutation of the marine vegetation anywhere
to be seen into fresh-water forms. They are as distinct now
as they were thousands of years ago, as is eloquently pointed
out in the following passage from Hugh Miller's *Footsteps of
the Creator* :—

> Along the green edge of the Lake of Stenness, selvaged by the
> line of detached weeds with which a recent gale had strewed its
> shores, I marked that for the first few miles the accumulation
> consisted of marine algæ, here and there mixed with tufts of stunted
> reeds or rushes, and that as I receded from the sea, it was the
> algæ that became stunted and dwarfish, and that the reeds, aquatic
> grasses, and rushes, grown greatly more bulky in the mass, were
> also more fully developed individually, till at length the marine
> vegetation altogether disappeared, and the vegetable *débris* of the
> shore became purely lacustrine,—I asked myself whether here, if
> anywhere, a transition flora between loch and sea ought not to be
> found? For many thousand years ere the tall gray obelisks of
> Stenness, whose forms I saw this morning reflected in the water,
> had been torn from the quarry or laid down in mystic circle on
> their flat promontories, had this lake admitted the waters of the
> sea, and been salt in its lower reaches and fresh in its higher. And
> during this protracted period had its quiet, well-sheltered bottom
> been exposed to no disturbing influences through which the delicate
> process of transmutation could have been marred or arrested. Here
> then, if in any circumstances, ought we to have had, in the broad
> permanently brackish reaches, at least indications of a vegetation

intermediate in its nature between the monocotyledons of the lake and the algæ of the sea; and yet not a vestige of such an intermediate vegetation could I find among the up-piled *débris* of the mixed floras, marine and lacustrine. The lake possesses no such intermediate vegetation. As the water freshens in its middle reaches the algæ become dwarfish and ill-developed ; one species after another ceases to appear, as the habitat becomes wholly unfavourable to it ; until at length we find, instead of the brown, rootless, flowerless fucoids and confervæ of the ocean, the green, rooted, flower-bearing flags, rushes, and aquatic grasses of the fresh water. Many thousands of years have failed to originate a single intermediate plant.

Besides sea-trout and yellow trout, the lower loch is said to contain flounders, cod, herrings, skate, whitings, eels, lythe, saithe, and gray mullet. There are no salmon now to be found in the Loch of Stenness. But in a book entitled *Present State of the Orkney Islands*, published in 1775, and reprinted in 1884, we are told that—

In this loch are abundance of trout, and in all probability there would be a good salmon fishing here, were it not that the mouth of the loch is so much choked up with sea-weed that the fish cannot get into it. What confirms this opinion is, that in some charters belonging to the gentlemen in the neighbourhood the salmon fishing in the loch is expressly reserved to the king as his exclusive right.

The yellow trout in Stenness and Harray are equal in quality to any in Scotland. But they are not nearly so plentiful as they ought to be ; nor, as a rule, do they rise freely. They have been taken as heavy as 6 lbs. But such a size is very rare, though individuals of 2 and 3 lbs. are not uncommon.[1] I have known one gentleman catch twelve trout in Harray in a few hours, weighing 13 lbs. ; and Mr. A. Irvine Fortescue of Swanbister, in answer to my printed queries about the trout fishing in the Loch of Harray, writes :—

Myself and friend once caught twelve and a half dozen, weighing 40 lbs., with fly, in four hours.

Mr. Fortescue states that, at times, the trout assemble in

---

[1] Since the above was written the handsomest yellow trout I ever saw was taken from the Loch of Stenness on a set-line. The weight was no less than 28 lbs. Mr. Malloch of Perth, the well-known fishing-tackle maker, made a beautiful cast from it.

dense shoals in some of the small bays of the Loch of Harray, and are, on such occasions, swept out in vast quantities by the net, and he is therefore of opinion that the use of the sweep-net should be prohibited in the Loch of Harray, as he considers it even deadlier than set-lines and set-nets. Mr. Fortescue mentions that, on the occasion when he and his friend caught the twelve and a half dozen, as above stated, they had come upon one of these shoals of trout, and he says that, with a net

The entire shoal might have been taken at one sweep, the result possibly a cart-load.

Sea-trout ascend to the Loch of Stenness and the other Orcadian lochs communicating with the sea, beginning in July and continuing throughout the autumn. The best place for sea-trout fishing in connection with the Loch of Stenness is called " The Bush," the term applied to the lower part of the stream on the seaward side of the Bridge of Waithe. I have known upwards of fifty sea-trout hooked there in a day by one rod, though, for want of a landing-net, only twenty of them were basketed. " The Bush " is a favourite resting-place for sea-trout before running up into the loch, and the most favourable time for fishing it is from half-ebb round to half-flood. A westerly wind is said to suit it best.

Before 1881 and 1882, when the Orkneys were constituted a Fishery District, and the usual bye-laws passed fixing estuaries, a close season, the meshes of nets to be used for the capture of fish of the salmon kind, and prohibiting certain methods of fishing, all kinds of destructive and improvident modes of fishing were commonly practised on the Loch of Stenness, and more particularly on the upper part of it, the Loch of Harray. Set-lines, set-nets, sweep-nets, and the otter, were in constant operation ; and, although the use of the otter and the fixed nets is now illegal, the " Harray lairds," as the small proprietors on the banks of the Loch of Harray are called, cannot be prevented, as the law at present stands, from using the sweep-net or set-lines, as they are udallers, and many of their properties have a frontage to the loch. No District Board has been formed for the Orkneys, nor is there any Angling Association for the protection and improvement of the fishings; and from what I saw and heard when in Orkney, I am by no means convinced that the statutory restrictions intended to prevent wasteful and improvident modes of fishing are much attended to on the Lochs of Stenness and Harray. Were they fairly fished and properly protected they ought to be equal to any lochs in the United Kingdom; and this is not merely my own opinion, after a pretty extensive acquaintance with these lochs, but that of every angler who has had much experience of them. In his admirable book on *The Orkneys and Shetland*, published in 1883, Mr. Tudor writes as follows of these two great lakes :—

For years, nets, set-lines, and the infernal poaching machine, the otter, have been used to such an extent that it is a wonder any trout have been left, but now the Orkneys have been formed into a Salmon Fishery district, set-lines and otters became illegal, and netting can no longer be carried out with the herring-net mesh, and in the reckless manner hitherto in vogue. In fact, if only the fish can be protected during the spawning season, these two lochs should, for angling, be second to none in Scotland.

To the same effect Mr. Sutherland Græme of Græmeshall, who has a large estate on the Mainland of Orkney, writes, in answer to my printed queries :—

I believe that if the lochs of Stenness and Harray were properly looked after and preserved by an Angling Association, they would be the finest fishing lochs in Scotland, both for sea and loch trout.

But without a District Board or an Angling Association, what is the use of statutory prohibitions of destructive and unfair modes of fishing? What are laws good for if there is no one to enforce them? They are a mere dead letter, not likely to be respected or observed by those whose interest, or fancied interest, it is to break them.

Mr. Heddle, the proprietor of the island of Hoy, an experienced angler, agrees with the views above expressed, and he stated to me when I was in Orkney that no good has, as yet, resulted from bringing the Orkneys under the operation

of the Salmon Fishery Acts of 1862 and 1868. No District
Board, no Association of Proprietors has been formed, no
prosecutions have been instituted—matters go on just as
before. With regard to the Lochs of Stenness and Harray,
he believes that nothing short of the killing of the spawning
fish and extensive ottering could have so much reduced the
fishing on such great expanses of water with such wonderful
natural capabilities. Fair fishing would never do it. Twenty-
one years ago his father and he killed so many fish in Stenness
in one day that they did not like to take any more. There
were between 100 and 200, all good-sized trout. Four years
ago he fished the same loch and got only about half a dozen
fish. One of these, however, was 2½ lbs.

Mr. Gould, chamberlain to the Earl of Zetland, corroborates
these views. He told me that the Acts had done no good as
regarded the great lakes of Stenness and Harray, in which
poaching was as rife as before the Acts were made to apply
to the islands. A clause should be put into an Act of
Parliament absolutely prohibiting ottering. Mr. Gould is of
opinion that the right of salmon fishing, or rather sea-trout
fishing, in the Lochs of Stenness and Harray belongs to the
Earl of Zetland or to the Crown. He maintains that the
Harray lairds are not udallers, and that their riparian rights
give them a title to yellow trout fishing only.

In the autumn of 1880 a public inquiry was held by the
Commissioners of Scotch Salmon Fisheries at Kirkwall,
Stromness, and the Bridge of Waithe, in connection with the
proposal to erect the Orkney Islands into a Fishery District,
and some interesting and important evidence was laid before
them about the fisheries in Stenness and Harray, and the
sea-trout fisheries in the Orkneys generally. With regard to
the size attained by the Orcadian sea-trout, one witness stated
that he had heard of one caught in a net, 21½ lbs. weight,
and had seen one of 12½ lbs.; and another witness stated
that he had seen one of 14 lbs. One of the witnesses
examined at Kirkwall said, that about six years ago there
was a curious epidemic among the trout in the Loch of

Harray, when most of the fish died. He went down to the banks of the loch one day and found them lying dead all along the shore. There was no appearance of any fungoid growth on any of the fish. The season had been a very hot and dry one. Next year there were very few fish. The majority of the witnesses examined agreed as to the evil effects of the destructive modes of fishing practised in Lochs Stenness and Harray, such as set-lines, sweep-nets, and fixed nets, otters, and the non-observance of any annual close time. In consequence of this the sea-trout and loch-trout are less numerous, and the individual fish are smaller in size than they used to be. In short, the tendency of the evidence taken by the Commissioners clearly proved the evil effects of allowing fishing unrestricted as to season or implements, and the necessity of imposing some restrictions. One witness deponed that he had seen eight or nine otters being used on the Loch of Harray one day, and the next day two on the Loch of Stenness. Another said that during the last five years there had been a marked falling off in the fishings, which he imputed to the use of sweep-nets, lines (each with several hooks) set during the night and drawn in the morning, and nets stretched and fixed across the whole breadth of the water above and below the Bridges of Waithe and Brogar, so as to intercept the passing fish. These nets have a small mesh, like herring-nets, and are set, not only in the lochs, but also across the burns running into them, where they do a great deal of mischief, especially during the spawning season. Another witness, who had then (1880) known the Loch of Stenness for thirty years, said, that when he first knew it there was nothing but fair fishing with rod and line. He also said that he had, long ago, killed thirty sea-trout with rod and line in that loch in three hours. They weighed from 3 lbs. downwards. Such a take would be impossible now owing to the otters, set-lines, and nets; but if a close time were enacted and enforced, and the lochs protected, such are their natural advantages that the fishings would recover in a few years.

APPENDIX B

Oysters and Mussels in the Shetland Islands.

Mr. Tudor, in his *Orkneys and Shetland*, published in 1883, writes as follows :—

The Shetlanders are said to have nearly exhausted the large whelks known as *buckies*, and to be fast destroying the mussel scalps, as they have already done the oyster-beds which previously existed in Cliff Sound and other places.

My recent visit to Shetland enables me to corroborate the truth of this statment, especially as regards oysters. Yet there can be no doubt that oysters were once plentiful and cheap, even within the memory of living man, and might again be so if judiciously cultivated and adequately protected. Mr. Anderson of Hillswick, a fish-curer and general merchant in Shetland, whose acquaintance with the fisheries ranges over a long series of years, sends me the following list of localities in Shetland which, he thinks, would be suitable for oyster culture, specifying those in which oysters are still found :—

1. Bressay Sound, on the east side, near the kirk ; west side, docks to Grimesta.
2. Dales Voe ; oyster spat was sown here by proprietor, Mr. Hay.
3. Laxfirth Voe should be an excellent place, also good trout fishing.
4. Wadbister Voe.
5. Catfirth Voe.
6. Dourye Voe.
7. Vidlin Voe.
8. Swining Voe.
9. Collafirth Voe (Delting).
10. Dales Voe   (do.)
11. Firths Voe.
12. Tofts Voe, near Mossbank.
13. Hamna Voe (Yell).   Fine trout taken here.
14. Burravoe   (do.)
15. Reafirth Voe (do.), or Mid Yell.
16. Basta Voe (Yell).   Here oysters are found.

17. Balta Sound (Unst).
18. Whalfirth Voe (Yell).
19. Lady Voe   (do.)   West Sandwick.
20. Collafirth Voe, Northmaven.
21. Quayfirth Voe   do.
22. Gluss Voe   do.
23. Garths Voe (Delting).
24. Voxter Voe   (do.),   and all round to Northmaven.
25. Hubens, near Foula Ness.
26. Ronas Voe.
27. Hanma Voe, Northmaven ; trout or salmon caught here
     some years ago, 14 lb. weight.
28. Urafirth Voe, Northmaven, near Hillswick.   Oysters found.
29. Hammers Voe.
30. Gunnister Voe.
31. Mangester Voe.
32. Roe Sound (Delting).   Here oysters have been found.
33. Burravoe, in Busta Voe.   Here also oysters are found.
34. Olnafirth Voe.
35. Gonfirth Voe.
36. Aiths Voe and East Burrafirth Voe.
37. Vementry, Clousta Voe, and Unifirth Voe.
38. West Burrafirth Voe.
39. Vaila Sound.
40. Gruting Voe.
41. Bixter Voe.   Here oysters are found.
42. Wiesdale Voe.
43. Stromness Voe.
44. Whiteness Voe.
45. Burra Isles.   Here oysters are found.
46. Troudra and Scalloway.

In his letter to me, enclosing the above list, Mr. Anderson writes as follows :—

I hope one possessed of capital may see the way to prosecute the oyster culture here ; it might become of immense importance to our country.

Of the localities mentioned by Mr. Anderson, I have personally visited Dales Voe, Aiths Voe, Laxo Voe, Catfirth Voe, Wadbister Voe, Bixter Voe, Basta Voe, Balta Sound, Stromness Voe, and some others, and I quite agree with him in thinking them well fitted for oyster cultivation.

I have received a good many communications in answer to

the printed queries on the subject of oysters and mussels in Shetland. One gentleman writes :—

I consider it most essential that the oyster-culturist should have a legal right to the beds, and also that he should be enabled to claim protection. Almost every voe in Shetland would be suitable for oyster culture, especially Basta Voe, Garths Voe, and Arna Voe.

Another states that—

The number of oysters has greatly decreased. I remember, as a boy, the women used to bring them to the houses and sold them for 1s. the 100. That would be in the early part of 1870. The Voe of Bixter has been completely dredged up. One of the neighbouring tenants made £500 one winter by dredging and exporting.

One of the principal proprietors in Shetland writes :—

The Burra Islands, near Scalloway, is the only place where a few oysters are now got. Oysters formerly were abundant in Basta Voe, North Yell, and sold at 1s. the barrel. But they were dredged up to the very last one.

The fishery officer at Lerwick states that there are no oyster beds or mussel scalps at present in Shetland which are regularly worked and yield a profit to their owners :—

Oysters have decreased, but the supply of mussels is about the same. Oysters were at one time got in considerable numbers near Burra Isle, but have been dredged out. It would be essential to have the protection of the law in some form.

He gives the following places as best suited for oyster or mussel culture—Basta Voe, Olnafirth Voe, Vaila Sound, Weisdale Voe, Burra Isle, etc. etc. A Lerwick merchant, thoroughly well informed in all matters relating to the fisheries, writes :—

Any oysters or mussels got in Shetland are taken up without any leave being asked from any one. But very few oysters remain. The number of oysters and mussels has diminished very considerably. There are a great many cases in which formerly productive oyster and mussel beds have been dredged out and destroyed. No steps are being taken to restore such beds. Protection is essential. I should say that all round Shetland there are places suitable for the culture of both oysters and mussels. But nothing will be done by proprietors or others to improve the present state of matters until the law assists them.

INDEX

THE END

www.ingramcontent.com/pod-product-compliance
Lightning Source LLC
Chambersburg PA
CBHW020356030726
47496CB00007B/2165